"You know we're doing everything we can, Valerie."

It wasn't what she wanted to hear from her boss. "I know about the search parties. They've come up with nothing. What about kidnapping? I want to be part of this investigation."

Gage's voice gentled. "You don't need me to tell you that you're much too involved in this...that you could wear blinders and not know it."

Valerie nodded, admitting to herself that this was probably true.

He then turned his attention to Guy Redwing. "How do you feel about Valerie becoming involved?"

Valerie looked at the face of the man beside her. A strong face that broadcast his ancestry. She didn't think about what that might mean for him. Didn't give a thought to the fact that he might feel she was in some way denigrating him by insisting she become involved in his investigation.

Guy Redwing paused a few moments. His expression remained stoic. "All help is welcome, Gage. We need to find that little girl."

CONARD COUNTY: CODE ADAM

New York Times Bestselling Author

RACHEL LEE

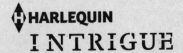

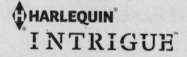

Recycling programs
for this product may
not exist in your area.

ISBN-13: 978-1-335-58272-0

Conard County: Code Adam

Copyright © 2023 by Susan Civil-Brown

For questions and comments about the quality of this book, please contact us at CustomerService@Harlequin.com.

Harlequin Enterprises ULC
22 Adelaide St. West, 41st Floor
Toronto, Ontario M5H 4E3, Canada
www.Harlequin.com

Printed in U.S.A.

Rachel Lee was hooked on writing by the age of twelve and practiced her craft as she moved from place to place all over the United States. This *New York Times* bestselling author now resides in Florida and has the joy of writing full-time.

Books by Rachel Lee

Harlequin Intrigue

Conard County: The Next Generation

Cornered in Conard County
Missing in Conard County
Murdered in Conard County
Conard County Justice
Conard County: Hard Proof
Conard County: Traces of Murder
Conard County: Christmas Bodyguard
Conard County: Mistaken Identity
Conard County: Christmas Crime Spree
Conard County: Code Adam

Visit the Author Profile page at Harlequin.com.

CAST OF CHARACTERS

Guy Redwing—Conard County Sheriff's detective. Native American. Leading team to find the missing child. Doesn't want some outside detective getting involved.

Valerie Brighton—Gunnison, CO, detective. Sister to May Chamberlain. Involves herself in the investigation of her niece's disappearance.

Gage Dalton—Conard County Sheriff. Approves Valerie Brighton's involvement in the investigation.

May Chamberlain—Teacher on sabbatical, mother of missing child.

Chet Chamberlain—Ob-gyn, father of missing child. May's ex-husband.

Philip Margolis—A man with a serious grudge against Chet Chamberlain.

Chapter One

"Lizzie's gone!"

From the moment Valerie Brighton had heard her sister May's sobbing voice on the telephone, Valerie had hit high gear. She'd quickly arranged for an indefinite leave from her job as a detective with the Gunnison, Colorado, police department, then hit the road for Wyoming with a couple of hastily packed suitcases.

Her two-year-old niece was missing. Vanished. May had said that search parties roamed Conard County looking for the child. There was no way Valerie could stay away. No way.

She passed through mountains with deep verdant valleys into the rolling range surrounding Conard City. Wide open, it was great ranch country, and it was vast. Except for those mountain ranges to the east and west, it seemed almost endless.

Keeping herself to just above the speed limit maddened her. She couldn't drive fast enough to suit herself. May needed her. Her niece needed her. Even though her badge would probably get her through

any traffic stop, the stop would still cost her time—
time she refused to spare.

What was that old problem she'd worked on in a
long-ago physics class? The one where they had cal-
culated the time saved by traveling over a long distance at one speed and compared it to traveling at a
much higher speed? The higher speed only saved a
few minutes, much to her surprise.

Just a few minutes. She had to keep reminding
herself of that as her foot tried to press more heavily
on the accelerator.

God, May must be living through an indescrib-
able hell.

Just about five miles before she reached Conard
City, she caught sight of a small bundle on the shoulder of the road. Her heart nearly stopped as she
jammed on the brakes and came to a skidding halt
on gravel. Her niece?

"Oh, please, God," she whispered. "Please. Not
my niece."

She jammed her black SUV into Park, then ran
back along the road to the white heap.

Not her niece. No. She started breathing again. A
dog. A medium-sized black-and-white dog, struck by
a car and appearing dead. She would have turned to
leave, but then the animal raised its head.

"Hell," she said to the empty spaces. "Hell." She
couldn't leave that poor dog like this. A sliver of sorrow managed to pierce the huge sense of anguish that
squeezed her heart.

Bending, heedless of her tailored black pantsuit,

she carefully lifted the dog, hearing it whimper. Poor thing. Poor, poor doggie.

She placed the injured animal in the back of her SUV and hit the road again, this time driving faster. Now she needed those few minutes. Every one of them. As much as that dog needed a vet.

Just as she spied the town before her, she saw a sign.

Mike Windwalker, DVM.

Valerie swore again at the inescapable delay and turned onto the rough gravel road leading to a large building labeled *Veterinary Hospital and Boarding*.

She braked on an unpaved parking lot and hurried inside. At the reception desk she said, "I found an injured dog on the roadside. He's in the back of my car."

There was no hesitation at the desk. A technician appeared immediately from the back and he hurried out to the car with her. With gentle hands, he checked the dog all over. Valerie waited impatiently.

"We'll get him inside," he told her. "You want to sign him over to us?"

"Sign?"

"Then we can take care of him, depending on what we can do. Or put him to sleep."

Valerie stomped down on her own impatience, allowing concern for the animal to creep in again. "No, I don't want to sign him over. I'll pay for his care, whatever it is."

Inside, the vet was waiting, and he regarded her with gentle dark eyes.

She signed several papers with an angry slash and left her cell phone number. "Any deposit?" she demanded. "Look, I've got to get to my sister. Her baby has disappeared."

The clinic grew suddenly silent, except for some dogs barking in the background.

"May Chamberlain," the vet said with a short nod of understanding. "Get on your way. We can worry about money later."

The dog disappeared into the back as fast as Valerie disappeared out the door.

May. She had to get to May. She had to help find her niece.

Chapter Two

May's house sat at the very edge of town, a large two-story brick structure with a front porch that was decorated with white pillars and white gingerbread. A few cars of various ages lined the street. Valerie pulled into the driveway behind her sister's blue Explorer.

Then she headed in the front door, unsurprised to see several women her sister's age surrounding May like broody hens. Probably keeping her company. Probably trying to steady her through this awful time.

The instant May saw Valerie, she rose from the black leather couch where she'd been seated and ran into her arms. May began sobbing, wrenching sobs that shook her entire body.

"Lizzie is gone," May wept, her voice almost smothered by worry and grief. "She's *gone*!"

Valerie held her tightly, wishing to God she could offer some comfort other than her presence. "You need to sit," she said quietly, feeling her sister's weakness, the way May clung to her as if for physical support.

"Come on," she prodded gently. "Please sit. It won't make the waiting and worrying any easier, but it'll keep you from collapsing."

Still shaking, May allowed herself to be guided back to the couch. "Val, I'm going out of my mind!"

Sitting beside her, Valerie took her sister's cold, trembling hands in hers. "I know you are, sweetie. I know you are."

May lifted her tear-stained face to look at her sister from reddened, swollen eyes. "She was gone when I woke this morning. Gone from her crib. They think she might have let herself out during the night. Oh my God, my poor Lizzie!"

The sobs renewed and Valerie wrapped her arms around her sister, holding her tight. Her own heart squeezed so hard that it hurt. "Where's Chet?" she asked eventually, referring to May's ex-husband.

"He's out with the search parties," one of the young women answered. "I'm Gina, by the way."

Valerie gave her a brief nod. "We went to school together, right?"

Gina nodded, her own eyes red-rimmed.

May demanded brokenly, "How could Lizzie have gotten out? How?"

"It happens," Valerie answered. "It happens." She knew it did. During her law enforcement career, she'd seen it happen a couple of times. Inquisitive or bored kids, knowing more about opening doors than their parents imagined. Always a terrifying situation.

"I can't bear to think of her out there all alone. It gets chilly at night and all she had on were her fuzzy pajamas."

May's sobs renewed but slowly they lessened. She'd spent all her energy crying. Eventually, she eased away from Valerie and grabbed a handful of tissues from a box on the glass-topped coffee table. The interior of the house, in contrast to the outside, was decorated in a modern style. Wedgwood blue paint covered the walls, giving color to an otherwise colorless room of black, white and chrome.

Valerie glanced down at herself and saw her suit jacket was pretty much decorated with black and white dog fur. A match for this room, she thought humorlessly. She clenched her hands, struggling to remain calm even as fear rattled her heart.

One of the women, also vaguely remembered from school days, brought a plate of store-bought cookies from the kitchen and set it on the table. Her name was Jenna Blair, Valerie seemed to remember. "Eat something, May. You need the energy to get through this."

Her sister could probably also use a pill or a shot to help her calm down. Valerie shook her head slightly. May wouldn't accept it. The sisters were both stubborn, sometimes to a fault.

She glanced at her watch and saw that night was approaching. So many hours since she'd left Gunnison. So many hours since May had called her after making the terrifying discovery. No one could even be sure how long Lizzie had been gone.

Night. A small child toddling out there without protection, without much-needed warmth as the night's inevitable chill deepened. Her mouth went dry with all the possibilities she'd been refusing to consider: the cold, coyotes. Other dangers, places she could fall into and hurt herself. Drowning in some creek, unable to get out of it.

She yanked her thoughts away from those paths. She couldn't afford to think this way or she'd be useless to May.

But she couldn't forget the last time she'd held Lizzie, a sweet-smelling little bundle of giggles and grins. A bit devilish, too. Pulling the upholstery buttons off an overstuffed chair. Leaning through the stair railing, calling out with glee. The kid in the bucket swing who couldn't seem to fly high enough. A little daredevil. Lizzie loved her thrills.

"You know," she said to May, "Lizzie is probably out there having a great time. You know how she loves an adventure."

May nodded but her face didn't brighten at all.

Maybe that hadn't been the smartest thing to say, Valerie thought. Reminding May of her daughter's mischievous nature wouldn't help. Nothing could help, least of all when she felt like shattering herself.

But she couldn't do that. May needed her to be strong right now.

"Isn't any cop keeping in touch?" she asked the room at large. "A family liaison or something?"

May spoke almost angrily. "What good will that do? I don't need another person trying to tell me not to worry."

"I was thinking more along the lines of keeping you posted about what's going on." Right then she knew she was going to have a problem with this two-bit sheriff's department. At least if Lizzie wasn't found soon.

THE LIAISON SHOWED up less than an hour later. Her name was Kerri Canady and she was accompanied by a fluffy white service dog.

Valerie eyed her with curiosity, thinking that dog indicated what might be an interesting story. Apart from that, she was annoyed that the woman arrived wearing a dark green uniform windbreaker, an obvious reminder of what was happening to the temperature outside. God, didn't anyone think?

Kerri squatted in front of May, her voice gentle.

"Mrs. Chamberlain, we haven't found Lizzie yet. But we're going to keep on looking through the night and we'll expand the search area."

May regarded her from dry eyes, her face ashen. "I can't believe you haven't found her yet."

"Kids, even little ones like Lizzie, can sometimes walk a surprising distance. We're also going to re-check the search area we've already covered. If she's out there, we'll find her."

May's voice rose. "*If?* Where else would she be? Where? She'll die of the cold tonight! You know that, don't you? You know that!"

"Kids," Valerie interjected, needing to offer a thread of hope, "are surprisingly resourceful. She probably got tired and crawled into some safe place to sleep. A place that's warm. A place that's harder to find." But the deepening night outside seemed to be creeping into her own heart, and her own expression of hope sounded hollow in her ears.

May's desperate eyes pinned her. "Do you really believe that?"

"I do," Valerie answered firmly even though she didn't. "I've known of it happening. There was a four-year-old. Nights were cold. After three days everyone was about to give up when one of the searchers found the boy ten miles from the campsite he'd left. Other than scratches, he was fine. Hungry and cold but fine. Still, he'd traveled *ten* miles."

May nodded jerkily. "Okay. Okay." Then she sank back into the depths. "She's gone," she whispered. "Gone."

Valerie looked at Kerri. "How many searchers do you have?"

One corner of Kerri's mouth lifted. "Half the damn county, seems like. People have been coming from everywhere."

"And the search radius?"

"We're expanding to ten miles right now. With all these helping hands pouring in throughout the day, we've got plenty of people out there."

Valerie nodded. She no longer felt quite as annoyed with the sheriff's department, but the feeling hadn't fully subsided. "How come it took you so long to get here?"

Kerri frowned slightly. "You know, I was dealing with the victim of a different kind of problem. As for everyone else, they're either searching or maintaining necessary patrols. If you have questions about how we're handling this, I suggest you talk to Detective Redwing. He's got oversight."

"Not the sheriff?" Valerie knew she was being difficult but didn't care. She knew how a police department operated. They couldn't just drop all their work to focus on a single task, no matter how urgent. But sitting here like this, unable to do anything, was edging her concern for May and Lizzie with a trickle of anger.

"The sheriff," Kerri said, "has oversight of *everything*. As you know." Then she rose from her squat and sat in a nearby chair. The service dog stayed right beside her.

Valerie turned to May. "It'll be okay." She wished she believed it.

Chapter Three

The next morning brought a bright blue sky that struck Valerie as a betrayal. As if the weather cared.

But last night had been chilly enough to be of major concern to those who believed a small child was lost out there. Despite the story she had told May, she knew all too well that such stories rarely had a happy ending. Such endings were exceptions to a nearly hard and fast rule.

Just after midnight, May had fallen asleep from sheer exhaustion. Her sleep was restless, though, filled with terrors that sometimes made her cry out. Small escape. Or maybe no escape at all. While she had slept, Valerie had grabbed naps as she could.

Valerie stood at the front window, watching the day brighten to an almost hard brilliance. Full of promises that ought to be painted in black, not blue.

She heard stirring behind her and saw that Kerri Canady was waking in the chair she'd used most of the night. Beside her, her service dog also stirred, sitting upright. On duty.

"Coffee?" Valerie asked.

"Love some, if you don't mind."

"I don't. I need it. Fuel."

Kerri smiled faintly. "The best kind."

"No news?"

"You've been there all night. You'd have heard my radio."

Valerie knew it to be true, but sometimes fear could make a person ridiculous. She was being ridiculous. She was also feeling resentful, angry and impatient. What the hell were all those people doing out there? Looking? Or getting too weary to see? Her stomach churned.

When the coffee finished brewing, she carried two cups to the living room and handed one to Kerri. "I should have asked if black is okay."

"It's great. Thank you."

Valerie resumed her watch of the street outside, waiting for some sheriff's vehicle that wasn't going to show.

She spoke again. "When does Gage Dalton get to the office?"

"Usually around eight."

Valerie nodded and glanced at her watch. Fifteen minutes. Her decision made, she dumped her coffee in the kitchen sink.

"I'm going out," Valerie said to Kerri. "If she wakes, tell May I'm checking on things."

Kerri simply nodded.

Dressed in a fresh black slack suit, one free of dog fur, she set out for the sheriff.

Gage Dalton's story was known all over town and Conard County, even to people who had been too young to have remembered it when it had happened. A former undercover agent for the DEA, he'd seen his wife and kids blown up by a car bomb that had been intended for him. That had also burned him badly.

When he'd arrived in Conard County, apparently a friend of the old sheriff, he'd been a man lost in a bleak abyss. Living in a room above Mahoney's bar, he'd established a nightly routine: one drink followed by an endless walk along empty night streets. Hate and despair had burned in his dark eyes, frightening away anyone who might have spoken to him.

Back then the locals had called him *hell's own archangel*.

Then Emmaline Conard, the local librarian, had drawn him steadily back into the light. Into the world of the living. Had brought smiles to his face.

Valerie was certain the grief had never left him, the guilt must have remained, but he'd reconstructed his life.

Now he was known as the new sheriff, despite all the years he'd held the position, but this county had loved the old sheriff too much to let go of him entirely. Now they loved their new sheriff, too. They certainly admired him.

But this would be the first time they met on equal footing, her being a cop, too. A detective.

One who wasn't going to sit on her hands, able to do nothing but try to comfort her sister.

One who was determined to get involved or there'd be hell to pay.

GUY REDWING SAT in the mobile command post, radios crackling around him, questions coming at him like annoying mosquitoes. No news yet.

He sipped the coffee someone had brought him. It was cold now, as cold as his heart. The little girl still hadn't been found. No trace of her anywhere.

A local Amber Alert had gone out yesterday, but no one held any hope that it would bring news. The child couldn't have wandered *that* far, far enough that someone who didn't know her might see her. The worst fear was that she was alone in the range that surrounded Conard City.

The sun was rising and hope was dying as a new day dawned. They'd keep looking but he was beginning to believe that they'd find Lizzie Chamberlain's body out there. When they found her.

But the longer the little girl remained missing, the more he began to have a darker thought: kidnapping. Like it or not, they were going to have to start looking at that possibility, even without a ransom note or phone call. And there could be other reasons besides a ransom for stealing a child, all horrifying to contemplate. As soon as he got to the office, he was extending the Amber Alert if Gage hadn't already.

He rose after the day became fully bright. He shook off fatigue and turned to his second-in-command, an experienced deputy named Connie Parish. "I need to get home and change. I probably smell like a wet dog that's been rolling in poop."

Connie smiled faintly. "Not quite that bad, Guy. But go. You'll be back just in time for the food train."

And train it would be, Guy thought as he stepped outside into the chilly air. People from all over would be showing up with food to lay out on long folding tables. As searchers switched out, coming in for a break, they'd be starving and cold. Exhausted, too.

And Maude, the owner of the City Café, would be arriving with yet another truckload of insulated carafes of coffee. Bless her.

At home in his small apartment, he showered and changed into a fresh uniform. He tied his long black hair back with a leather thong. One thing he refused to get rid of.

Despite his promotion to detective, he still wore the uniform of a deputy. He was Native American and had met prejudice all his life, but that uniform helped a bit to grease the wheels in his professional dealings with the people he was sworn to protect. People he was sworn to serve who hated him merely because he wasn't White. The irony didn't escape him.

Nor did a bitter anger, which he tamped down as far as he could. It rose again when he faced overt prejudice, but he'd learned to keep a smooth face even when he wanted to punch someone. Life's lessons well and painfully learned.

Some among his own family didn't approve of him either. They saw him as a sellout.

Straddling the fence could be painful sometimes.

Then he shook his head, grabbed his windbreaker and headed for his official Suburban, a tan monster covered with road dust, in need of a good washing. The words *To Serve and Protect* seemed to mock him from where they were painted on the vehicle's side. Yeah. Okay then.

He rubbed grit from his tired eyes and told himself to quit the pity party. He'd made his choices and he lived with them. This BS was emerging only because he was so weary and worried.

Before he'd even backed out of his driveway, his radio crackled to life with his call sign. He was too tired to feel even a small lift of hope as he heard the dispatcher, Velma.

"You better get to the office," Velma said in her smoke-roughened voice. "Seems like there might be a little problem. I just know Gage wants to see you yesterday."

"Hell," he said, not caring if Velma heard it, not caring if every police radio for miles around heard it. *What now?*

VALERIE WAS CERTAIN that she was adding to the unpleasantness of Gage Dalton's morning, but she didn't care. She was past caring about anything except getting her niece back from the clutches of wild nature, or the clutches of some kidnapper.

Because she couldn't ignore the possibility of kidnapping, not when so many people were out there looking at the area around the town and into the scrub that surrounded it.

Her niece wasn't out there. Lizzie was lost, all right, but after the cold night just past, the idea of a kidnapping offered some hope, meager as it was. If anyone found Lizzie out there now amongst the grasses, in the uneven and treacherous terrain, they weren't apt to find her alive.

"It's got to be a kidnapping," she said, aware of Detective Redwing sitting beside her as they both looked at Sheriff Dalton across his desk. "No one's seen any sight of her. No clue as to her whereabouts."

Dalton's face had been burned on one side, shiny with old scar tissue that kept him from moving one side of his mouth and the eyebrow above one eye. It was a constant, scalding reminder to those who saw him. It was the face that must remind him every morning, as he stood before the bathroom mirror, of the wife and children he had lost through betrayal of his true identity.

But Gage had clearly learned to live with it. Learned to live with the pain that made him wince sometimes when he moved.

"You know we're doing everything we can, Detective." Acknowledging her experience.

It wasn't what she wanted to hear. "I know about the search parties. They've come up with nothing. What about kidnapping?"

He leaned forward, wincing, and picked up a pencil, tapping the eraser end on his desk. "There are a few problems with that."

"There's one hell of a big problem with all of this." Her hands tightened. She was not about to be side-lined or dismissed.

"I don't disagree. But there's no evidence of an intruder in your sister's house. None. So we're left with a problem, as in how did anyone remove that child from her crib?"

Good question, much as Valerie hated to admit it. "We need to investigate the possibility anyway. And I want to be part of that investigation."

"You're talking about some truly ugly things here. You're a detective. You don't need me to tell you that."

She closed her eyes briefly, hating what he hadn't said. That mothers *do* sometimes kill their own children. That fathers too often kidnapped them after a divorce. To get even. To assuage the bitterness and anger that could come from both rejection and from losing full custody. There would have to be an investigation of both May and her ex-husband.

His voice gentled. "You also don't need me to tell you that you're much too involved in this. That you could wear blinders and not know it. Like right now, you're sitting there convinced that neither May nor Chet could be involved."

He was right and she prickled a bit, but she knew something else. "I'll look under every rock. Right now *everyone* is a suspect."

Gage nodded slowly and turned his attention to

Guy Redwing. "How do you feel about Valerie becoming involved?"

Valerie looked at the face of the man beside her. A strong face with high cheekbones that broadcast his ancestry. She didn't think about what that might mean for him. Didn't give a thought to the fact that he might feel she was in some way denigrating him by insisting she become involved in his investigation. Never thought he might attribute her determination to a prejudice against the Indigenous people. Never thought that he might believe she was questioning his abilities *because* he was Native American.

Since yesterday, she had gone far past any kind of political correctness.

Guy Redwing paused a few moments. His expression remained stoic. "All help is welcome, Gage. We need to find that little girl."

"Well then," Gage said, dropping his pencil. His dark gaze bored into Valerie. "You need to understand one thing, Detective Brighton. *Guy* is the detective in charge of this case."

Outside on the street, a cold breeze freshened the air with threat. The unfeeling blue sky remained.

Guy Redwing put his uniform Stetson on his head. Tan like the rest of his uniform except for the dark green official jacket. Tall. Standing straight.

"You're a detective," she said to Guy Redwing. "Why do you still wear a uniform?"

"Look at my face," he said flatly.

It was then she began to understand. But she still

didn't care. "No other detective to help with this case?"

"Not right now. Our other detective, Callum Mc-Cloud, is away in Boston. You're stuck with *me*."

She gave a short nod. "How much experience do you have?"

"In law enforcement? Quite a few years. As a detective? I'm sure it's not as much as *you* have."

THE ANGER BURNED in Guy once again. Questioning his ability to manage this case by himself? There could be only one reason.

She was a tall, slender woman in crisply tailored clothes that were very much out of place here. Blond-haired, blue-eyed and pretty, the epitome of White.

Now he'd have to deal with her sense of superiority, especially given her longer experience with being a detective. He'd have to deal with her emotional involvement in this case. As if the case weren't difficult enough. He squared his broad shoulders, reminding himself that this was all about one small child. That child mattered more than anything.

"As for kidnapping," he said, "I've been considering it. But the search is going to continue whether you think it's a waste of time or not. No stone unturned. You said it yourself."

She answered with a brisk nod. "I wouldn't want the search stopped. There's always a chance…"

He drew a deep breath and blew it out between his lips. "We've got to question the people most directly involved. Are you up to it?"

"I'm not sure May is up to questioning, honestly. As for Chet, I have no idea. He's been out searching, I was told."

"He is. But what about *you*?"

She didn't answer him.

Now came the part Guy had spent the better part of yesterday and last night hoping to avoid. Questioning the parents. *God!*

He spoke again. "I'll take the lead. It'll be easier on you." It would make it easier for him, too, not having her intervene, perhaps encouraging certain answers.

Again she didn't reply to him. He hadn't expected her to.

CHET CHAMBERLAIN WAS a man of moderate height with a thick head of brown hair and eyes that were often gentle. As an OB-GYN, he had a great many opportunities to be gentle. Usually he was impeccably dressed for this area, in neatly pressed clothes that were Western enough to fit in.

Right then he was grungy, his jeans covered with blades of dry grass and small twigs, his chiseled face smeared with some dirt he must have gotten on his hands. As he sat on the black leather couch, one arm wrapped around an ashen May, he looked like a man reaching the end of his tether. And May looked like the spitting image of her sister.

"Anything change?" he asked Guy Redwing as soon as Guy crossed the threshold. Then he spied Valerie. "Hi, Val. May was hoping you'd come."

"Nothing's changed," Guy answered. He didn't sit until Chet waved him to a nearby chair, also black leather but with chrome legs. "Except that we're considering a new line of inquiry."

Valerie had already taken another chair. Her hands were twisted together, Guy noted. Why had she wanted to be part of this interview? It was going to tear her apart.

"I need to ask you both some questions," Guy said, returning his attention to Chet and May. "I know this will be difficult, but I've still got to ask them."

Chet nodded, his jaw tightening. "Ask. Val?"

"She's part of the investigation now," Guy answered. "Working with me. Any objection?"

May spoke, her voice tremulous. "I want her to be part of it if she's willing."

Guy managed a faint smile. "She demanded it. Her willingness isn't in question."

"What are *your* questions?" Chet demanded. "Do you want to know if one of us did something awful to Lizzie?"

May drew a sharp breath. "Are you kidding me?"

"We're looking into the possibility of kidnapping," Guy answered, evading the ugliest question now that May had brought it up herself. He had his answer to that one, for now. "The questions aren't going to be pleasant for you, but we need every possible bit of information to help find Lizzie."

May sagged again into the crook of Chet's arms. "I'd never hurt my baby. Neither would Chet."

Guy looked at Valerie Brighton. Her face had grown paler, but he saw no anger there. Okay. At this point she wasn't going to interfere with necessary questions. He turned back toward the couple on the couch. *He* needed to ignore the ache in his heart for these parents—to focus instead on his ache for the child caught in all of this.

Chet spoke. "Saying it isn't going to be enough, May. They have to ask questions, if there's any possibility that Lizzie was kidnapped. Or..."

He left the thought unfinished, but Guy realized the doctor was getting the full picture of the possible suspicions that might be directed their way. Chet's face had hardened, and his posture had grown more protective of May.

Guy changed tack. "Has anyone gotten seriously angry with either one of you recently?"

They both shook their heads.

Guy continued. "Anyone at all who might hold a grudge?"

Chet answered. "Not that I know of. May?"

"I can't imagine. Anything's possible, I guess." Tears began to roll down her face again. "Why would anyone steal our little girl?"

"That's what we need to find out," Valerie said, speaking for the first time. "Anything at all you can think of."

Apparently neither of them could.

Guy changed tack again. "When did you last see Lizzie, Mrs. Chamberlain?"

"I already told you that!"

"We need to go over it again. We're looking at everything from a different angle this time. So please, just tell me when last you saw her."

"When I put her to bed at eight. When I sat reading her a story and singing a lullaby. She was asleep when I left the room. I checked in on her maybe an hour later before I went to bed."

She shook her head and another tear trickled down her cheek.

"And you, Dr. Chamberlain?"

Chet's face had grown even harder. "Three days ago, when I stopped by to see her."

Guy nodded. "Is that your usual visitation schedule?"

This time Chet's voice cracked a little. "No. I took a chance. May and I disagreed about me just dropping in, but it was nothing major. She understands that I love Lizzie. May?"

"It's true. I felt like he was disrupting Lizzie's schedule. I can't have this pop-in-and-pop-out happening any old time. I told Chet he should at least call first."

Guy nodded. "Raising a child, especially one who's still not yet three, can be challenging and tiring."

May went from teary-eyed to angry. "Who cares?"

"It's a full-time job, and I hear the Terrible Twos can be fatiguing."

"She wasn't terrible. Ever."

"But when do you have time for *yourself*?"

LISTENING TO THESE questions filled Valerie with both anger and sorrow. She knew why they needed to be asked, but she hated that they were being directed at her sister as if May were capable of mistreating Lizzie.

"You know when it was hard?" May demanded. "Her infancy when she had colic. When I felt like a failure because there was nothing I could do to help her. When I walked the floor for hours in the middle of the night listening to her cry."

"Difficult," Guy agreed. "But time for you?"

"Day care for four hours three times a week. It gives me time to do the things I need to do, it gives me time to exercise my mind, to just relax or whatever. Oh, I had my own time, Detective."

Guy pulled a notebook from his pocket and flipped through a few pages. There was more, Valerie knew. Much more. Her hands ached from clenching them. From fighting the urge to go to May.

"You say you discovered she was missing at around seven a.m. Is that right?"

"God, yes. The instant I opened my eyes I knew something was wrong. She always woke me around six. She never lets me sleep late."

"So you heard nothing at all? No one moving in the house, no unusual sounds from Lizzie?"

"Nothing," May said, her voice stretched tight. "Not one peep." She shook her head. "Not a thing. I don't understand why! I should have heard her making some kind of noise. If someone took her, she should have made *some* sound at being disturbed.

She's at the point where she's afraid to be away from me, even when I take her to day care. She always cries."

"That's a normal stage," Chet said. "Normal. Right now she cries when I take her home with me. It doesn't last long, but she *cries*."

Oh, God, Valerie thought. This was getting worse and worse. It sounded as if May might be concealing something. Then came the most fearful question of all.

Guy asked it. "But you said yesterday that you have a baby monitor, right? Could it have been turned off?"

"It's on all the time!"

And there it was, a hole in her claim to have heard nothing at all, not Lizzie crying or any other sounds. God in heaven. Guy would be suspicious now, and justifiably so. Now Valerie was clinging to the hope that her sister couldn't be a monster.

"How often do you change the batteries?"

"The units are rechargeable. They beep to tell me the charge is getting low."

"So none of that?"

May shook her head. Now Chet was staring at her as if doubt were creeping into him as well.

Guy rose. "Mind if Detective Brighton and I take a look at them?"

May shrugged. "Go ahead."

Valerie rose with Guy and walked with him to Lizzie's room. The bedding in the crib was rumpled, the blanket thrown back as if the girl had been *taken*, not as if she had climbed out on her own. She pointed to it with a finger and Guy nodded.

God, she hoped she wasn't helping to deal a blow to May.

He found the monitor near the crib and lifted it, studying it. Then he summoned Valerie over with a crook of his finger. He'd slid the back off the monitor and Valerie stared into an empty space.

"Someone took out the battery," she murmured. "Oh, sweet Mother Mary."

She looked into Guy's strong face and for the first time saw past his impassivity. Pain filled his dark gaze.

"Kidnapping."

VALERIE GAVE HER sister a hug before she and Guy departed. He spoke.

"I'm going to send my team to knock on doors. They got nothing from the neighbors yesterday, at least the ones who were still home. A lot of folks were out in the search parties. But maybe someone will have remembered something if we jog them again."

"Maybe. Listen, I need just a minute to make a phone call."

"Go ahead." A phone call? At a time like this when he could almost feel the pain and anger that enveloped her?

Then she surprised him when she lifted her cell phone to her ear.

"Hi, this is Valerie Brighton. I brought in a small

black-and-white dog yesterday. The stray hit by a car? How's he doing?" She listened, then said, "Do it. I'll cover it." As she disconnected, she saw him staring at her. "A dog I found by the roadside. Broken hip. He's going to need surgery."

Well, that gave him a whole new spin on this woman who seemed both demanding and dubious of him. In the midst of all that must be tearing her apart, she had rescued a dog, had brought her to the vet and was now ensuring he received proper treatment.

Maybe there was a generous soul beneath all those roiling emotions, a soul that could save a dog despite everything. That, however briefly, could spare a little attention for an injured animal.

His opinion of her climbed a notch or two. "I'm going to check in with the command post. Then let's get some coffee while we discuss next steps."

She gave him a brief nod.

MAUDE'S DINER, as the City Café had been known for years, wasn't very busy. Just a few retirees too old to join the search. Coffee was easy to come by, delivered in thermal carafes that recently had replaced the individual cup-by-cup service. Maude's daughter Mavis, a clone of her stout and usually angry mother, had insisted on it. No time to waste pouring bottomless cups of coffee at all the tables.

Guy shoved a menu toward Valerie. "Get some breakfast. You'll need the energy. When was the last time you ate?"

"None of your business." But she hadn't eaten a thing since her departure from Gunnison. Fear and worry were good appetite suppressants. She took the menu, seeking something that wouldn't roil her stomach more.

Guy chose a double serving of biscuits and gravy. Valerie selected pancakes, the only thing that looked bland enough to swallow. She couldn't even face eggs. It was all about energy anyway.

She was surprised when she received a double order of the pancakes. She looked up into the face of Mavis. "I didn't order a double."

Mavis frowned. "I heard you. Eat as much as you can. Long day ahead." Then she stomped off.

Valerie stared at the heap of pancakes then looked at Guy. He shrugged. "She's right."

Then she studied her overly full plate, evading his gaze, which reflected concern, and she was sure some of it was about her. Of course. He didn't want her on this case and he had no idea what kind of problem she might become. Too bad.

For her own part, she honestly wasn't certain how objective she might manage to be. It was a good thing, though she hated to admit it, that she wasn't the lead on this one. Even though she wanted to batter her way through every obstacle at any cost.

Which made her a loose cannon.

She forced herself to eat despite all the worries and emotions careening around inside her. With each mouthful her stomach began to fill and the sugary syrup hit her bloodstream, energizing her.

"Okay," he said when he'd cleaned his whole plate and Valerie had eaten three quarters of hers. He poured them both fresh cups of coffee. "How many kidnapping cases have you worked?"

"None." But she *had* worked on a case where the mother had killed her child. She suppressed a shudder. *Not May.*

"Tell me more about Chet," he suggested. "He's a doctor, right?"

"Obstetrician. He shepherds mothers through their pregnancies and delivers their babies. He's fond of saying that his are the first hands that hold a newborn."

"He's proud of that?"

Valerie bridled. "He should be. Delivering a baby is an important role."

Guy shrugged one shoulder. "I didn't say anything was wrong with it."

Valerie sat sipping the hot coffee. Mavis stomped by to remove their plates.

Guy's gaze remained steady. This man, Valerie realized, wasn't going to give an inch.

"So," he said presently, "what brought about the divorce?"

It was Valerie's turn to shrug. "They'd been married five years. They seemed happy. Then May got pregnant."

"Joyous?"

"At first." Val took a napkin from the dispenser and began folding it aimlessly. God, she hated to talk about this. To become a witness, rather than a detective. But there was no escaping it. She shredded the napkin, trying to suppress her inner turmoil.

Guy spoke quietly. Almost gently. "I know this is hard."

"I was on the outside looking in," she told him defiantly. "Anything I say isn't gospel."

A brief nod. "Got it."

Valerie sighed, then stuck her toes in the water. "Chet's job has irregular hours. Babies don't get born on a schedule. He's not, as he's said, one of those doctors who will set up Caesarians to make a convenient schedule either for himself or the mother. He wants those babies to come to a natural full term. Unless there are complications, of course. So he can be called out at any hour of the evening or night for a delivery or a problem with a pregnancy."

Guy nodded again. "I can understand that."

"Well, May didn't seem to have a problem with that. At least not until she became pregnant. Then she started complaining to me about how little he was home."

"Okay."

Valerie's jaw had clenched. She forced herself to relax it before she gave herself a major headache. "It got worse after Lizzie was born. Chet had his regular office hours, of course, but he also had all those urgent calls to deal with. May felt she was the *only* one taking care of Lizzie. The *only* one who paced the floors at night with a colicky baby."

Valerie grabbed another napkin and began to treat it like the first. God, this was killing her. Her niece was out there somewhere but here she sat playing witness. With every word she felt as if she were betraying her sister.

"It wasn't true, of course," Valerie said, her hands tightening until her knuckles turned white. "Chet was there as much as he could be. But I guess that was the problem. Anyway, she felt abandoned and divorced him."

"There was a custody fight? I heard something about it through the grapevine."

"Double damn," Valerie said vehemently, hating this man and his questions. "When do I get to stop being a witness?"

Guy leaned back in his chair, his gaze unwavering. "Would you ask these questions in a similar case that didn't involve your sister?"

The words felt like a slap in the face, all the worse because she knew he was right. It mattered now, all of it mattered. He was just being a good detective, despite her initial doubts, and she should give him credit for that.

"All right. There *was* a brief custody fight. Chet wanted joint custody. May argued against it, talking about Chet's hours and how he'd have to hire a nanny to take care of Lizzie. She didn't want her daughter being raised by a stranger. She didn't want Lizzie's life to be upended every six months."

"And she won."

"Obviously."

Valerie closed her eyes, feeling her chest squeeze until she thought she might not be able to breathe.

She'd done it. She'd given both of them a motive, especially Chet. She hated herself.

Then her eyes popped open and she looked straight at Guy. "So tell me, Detective Redwing, just what good would it serve either of them to kidnap Lizzie? How hard would it be to conceal my niece in this town? Impossible. And if either of them put Lizzie in another's care, how often could they see that child? What's more, May's statement in court mitigates against that. She doesn't want Lizzie being raised by a stranger."

NONE OF IT mitigated against murder, however, Guy thought as they left the restaurant. Revenge? A deep grudge? Especially on the part of Chet. Gentle obstetrician he might be, but he'd been denied joint custody. Then to be told he didn't have the right to just drop in to see Lizzie? That had to have angered him. But enough to kill a child just to deprive May of it? *If I can't have it, neither can you.*

It wouldn't be the first time.

Anger churned in him. But he had to give props to Valerie Brighton. She'd given him as much as she knew because, as a detective, she understood its importance. Even though she had known where it might lead.

"Thank you," he said as they crossed the street toward the sheriff's office. "I know that wasn't easy." It hadn't been. She probably displayed a totally impassive face when she was working, a detective needed one, but she hadn't been impassive as a witness. He'd seen the play of terrible emotions run across her face. The awareness of what she might be doing. She was a strong woman.

"I need to go out to the command post," he said. "Check up on things."

"I'll come along. I'd like to see."

Of course she would want to make sure they weren't handling the matter like a bunch of rubes. That must be her opinion or she wouldn't have forced her way into this investigation. As a detective, she'd known better than to do so because she was personally involved.

Then he caught himself. More eyes, more ideas, might be useful.

THE MOBILE COMMAND CENTER, such as it was, had been positioned not far from the Chamberlain house in a grassy area, still browned from winter. He led Valerie inside and introduced her to Connie's replacement, a deputy named Sarah Ironheart. Sarah had a bit of a storied background, too, having years ago broken up a bar fight started because some locals objected to the presence of a Native American man. Sarah, herself partly Indigenous, had broken up the fight with a well-timed shotgun blast into the air. Later she had married the man, Gideon Ironheart, who was the long-lost brother of Micah Parish, also a deputy. Micah had his own stories to tell about the bigotry around here, although it had lessened somewhat since his day. Lessened but not vanished.

The extensive Parish family, however, had achieved

a measure of acceptance through their long years in law enforcement. Connie, who had been in the command post earlier, had married Micah Parish's eldest son.

That acceptance did not entirely extend to Guy, a relative newcomer whose roots lay in a reservation. He figured he'd always be something of an outsider around here but had long since resigned himself to it.

It is what it is.

"Good setup," Valerie remarked after she and Sarah had been introduced.

Sarah smiled. "It's pretty good, Detective."

"Valerie, please. Or Val if you prefer." Valerie pointed to the screens, one in particular. "What's that?"

"A GPS map of where the searchers have been. Cell phones are good for something besides calls, texts and surfing the web. I'm sure you know that. Anyway, all the searchers have been advised to turn on their mobile data so we can track them."

Valerie pulled over a chair and looked. "The search area looks blocky."

Sarah nodded. "Uneven ground, uneven pace. Guy?"

"We're extending the radius again today. Have the K-9s found anything?"

Sarah shook her head. "Not a trace."

Valerie exchanged looks with Guy. He returned a brief nod.

Kidnapping.

FEELING ALMOST ILL, Valerie left the command post with its monitors and humming, crackling radios. Outside, she paused to draw several deep breaths.

"Are you okay?" Guy asked quietly.

"Trying to be. At this point the only damn I give is for my niece. For Lizzie. And I'm not liking the chances."

"There's always a chance," he said firmly. "A better one if she hasn't been in the dark and cold all night. Someone could well be giving her decent care."

She looked at him from eyes that felt swollen, although no tears fell. "But *why*?" The obvious question.

"If we knew that, we'd know where to look."

"The obvious answer," she retorted. "Maybe this person will get in contact soon. Give us some kind of direction."

"I hope to God he or she does. The sooner the better."

ETTA MARGOLIS FOUND an envelope in her mailbox that afternoon. She regularly walked the half mile to the rural mailbox at the end of her rutted drive to collect the mail, mostly advertising flyers and the few monthly bills. This time there was a hand-addressed envelope. She barely looked at it and curiosity touched her only slightly.

She lived on a small piece of land outside of town, a parcel cut from a larger ranch, originally intended for the family of the rancher's son.

That family no longer lived there, having ske-daddled to a bigger city with more opportunity. The rancher, who'd fallen on tough times, had been only too glad to rent the house to Etta and her ex-husband for a song. A property he now didn't have to maintain.

Etta had lived there alone since her divorce, and the maintenance was more than she could handle alone. She lived in expectation of being evicted.

She also lived with terrible grief over the loss of her only child, a boy who'd been stillborn. Her grief and her husband's drunken anger, an anger that blamed her and her doctor both for the child's death, had ripped them apart. He had offered her no com-fort as she'd wept and ached—just his fury. For two years they had had no contact and she wanted it that way. His anger, his blame, had been intolerable in the midst of her bottomless grief.

Once back at the ramshackle house, she recog-nized her ex's handwriting on the envelope. God, she wanted nothing to do with that man ever again. She tossed it unopened into the trash can outside the house, where it would disappear beneath cof-fee grounds and food scraps and eventually into the compost heap.

Like the rest of her life.

Chapter Four

Valerie stopped by her sister's house. May, her blond hair now stringy, was surrounded by friends again. She looked up eagerly as Valerie entered.

"No news," Valerie told her immediately, wishing she could offer more. Her sister's anguish was unbearable, her own nearly so. "I'm sorry. We're working every angle. I just came home to change into better shoes before we start pounding the pavement. Do you need anything?"

"Only my baby," May answered, her voice breaking.

Valerie knelt before her, taking her hands, aching so much for May and Lizzie that she didn't dare let it show for fear of upsetting May even more. Someone *had* to offer hope. "Everything is being done. I can promise you that. Where's Chet?"

"A delivery needs his attention," May said almost bitterly. "There's always somebody else's baby." The unspoken words were there, though. *Never enough time for* our *baby*.

Valerie wondered how Chet could even manage to

deliver a baby under these circumstances. Or maybe he was escaping into work? Or escaping May's grief and fear?

She didn't know Chet well enough to judge.

She exchanged her dressy black shoes with two-inch block heels for black flats. Police shoes. Her feet didn't always like being shoved into the toe box of ladies' shoes and coming events might require her to run or travel over rough terrain.

When Valerie emerged from her bedroom, she found that Kerry Canady and her dog had been replaced by another liaison officer, a pretty young woman named Artie Jackson.

"Artie is short for Artemis," the deputy said as she rose to shake hands with Valerie. "I'll do my best to take care of May."

"I know you will." As would May's friends, who kept coming as if in shifts.

Then she stepped outside and found Guy Redwing waiting, leaning against his Suburban. Under other circumstances she might have thought he was an extremely handsome man. Under the current ones, she barely noticed.

"There are other people who might have a motive," she said as he pulled the vehicle away for the curb.

"Plenty, I imagine, once we start thinking about it."

"May and Chet know a lot of people, what with him being a doctor and her being a schoolteacher."

"Absolutely. Then there are all the day care workers. It doesn't take much to create a grudge in some people."

She felt his glance touch her briefly.

"It's going to be a long day," he remarked. "Even with other deputies helping with the questioning."

A long day indeed, especially when accompanied by worry and fear.

By FOUR THAT AFTERNOON, they'd talked to a lot of people, from neighbors to other acquaintances and the day care staff. All professed to be unaware of anyone who disliked May or Chet. Anyone who might have reason to nurse a grudge. No one had seen or heard anything.

No threat for ransom had arrived either, no phone call, no note.

Almost reluctantly, Valerie joined Guy for coffee and a meal at the diner. She didn't want to eat but knew she must. Lack of sleep was beginning to catch up with her. As well as anyone, she understood the importance of a clear head.

"We're stuck," she said bluntly as she finished a meal she hardly tasted.

"At the moment," he agreed.

Weary or not, Valerie still possessed her temper. "At the *moment*?" she demanded. "We've got nothing, no leads at all. Even the K-9s couldn't find a trace."

"We have a whole lot of people who all said the same thing, as was to be expected. Any one of whom might be lying or shading the truth."

She dropped her fork and nearly glared at him. "How the hell do we find that out? Are you going to do background checks on everyone in this town, in this county?"

His jaw tightened. "Those checks have already begun. Do you take me for a fool?"

He spoke mildly enough, but Valerie could see the anger burn in his dark eyes. After a few moments, she looked down at her half-empty plate. "No," she said finally. "No."

"Good, because I'm not. You may be a big-town detective, but I know this county, this town. I've been policing it for years. How long have you been away from here, *Detective*?"

Except for brief visits over the last twelve years, she'd lost touch with this area, especially the people. She barely remembered even her high school friends. Presently she said, "I apologize, Detective."

"Try calling me Guy. And I'll call you Valerie. Maybe we'll get some equality going here. As much as you can give an Indian, anyway."

Ouch. She turned her head to look out the big window beside them. People walking by as if everything were normal while May's life was one of torture. The whole world should be weeping. "I wasn't thinking that."

Or had she been? God knew prejudice against Native peoples was strong in this part of the country. Had she been harboring some without realizing it? But bigotry was an insidious thing, invisible to those who didn't suffer due to it.

She looked at him again, wondering about herself. "I'm sorry if I made you feel that way."

"I'm used to it."

A part of her pried itself away from her reaction to Lizzie's disappearance. She nearly winced at how Guy must be feeling. "What I was thinking, consciously anyway, was that this is a small department compared to what I work with now."

"Inexperienced," he corrected.

"Maybe."

"We deal with everything here," he said. "Everything. Maybe just not the quantity of cases you're used to."

Valerie nodded slowly. "I'm not exactly an expert on kidnapping."

He shrugged one shoulder. "Who is? With the possible exception of the FBI."

"Maybe they should be called in?"

"Not yet. A bunch of suits out here wouldn't be welcomed. The clams would rather suffocate."

In spite of herself, she smiled faintly. "You're probably right."

"I know I am." He picked up the check. "On me. Expense account. Then you should get yourself back to your sister's and try to get some sleep. I know it won't be easy, but we'll do better with fresh brains."

Valerie couldn't disagree, but she wondered if she'd be able to sleep at all.

GUY WATCHED VALERIE walk into the Chamberlain house. Well, the woman hadn't been as much of a pain as he'd expected. Professional in every way during their interactions with folks around here. But she needed to ditch that suit. Everyone looked at her dubiously, as if she wore a stamp that said *outsider.*

Instead of heading home himself, however exhausted his brain might be feeling, he went to the office to check in.

Gage Dalton was still there, keeping an eye on everything. Apparently he couldn't give up and find his bed yet either.

"No luck?" Gage asked when he saw Guy.

"Not a damn thing. If anyone has any suspicions, they're not saying a word."

"Must be the first time in this county's history that the grapevine hasn't been working overtime." Gage rubbed his eyes. "How's this Valerie Brighton working out?"

"Totally professional. Impressive under the circumstances."

Gage nodded. "I was concerned about that. I bet you were, too. Unfortunately, other than her personal involvement, I couldn't find a reason to tell her no. I suspect she'd just have gone off on her own. We don't need that."

Guy shrugged. "No one would have talked to her anyway. They don't know her anymore."

"And she sticks out in that suit," Gage said, echoing Guy's earlier thought. *Not one of us*, it would appear to folks. "I hoped that her connection to May and Chet might get her somewhere, though. Sympathy."

"Nope. Not yet anyway. And there's a downside to that connection. Who'd want to tell her that some-one hated her sister or former brother-in-law? Some things might be said elsewhere, but not to her face."

"Too true." Gage raised his one mobile eyebrow. "You need to hit the sack. Hell, *I* need to hit the sack. We'll be no good to anyone."

Reluctantly, Guy headed back to his small apart-ment. Just big enough for a bachelor. Needed some work, though. Maybe he'd get to it eventually.

Sleep eluded him for a while. He put on some soothing music and settled into a recliner, hoping his brain would stop spinning at high speed. He didn't want to let go of the problem. He couldn't stop think-ing about Lizzie. That poor little girl.

He closed his eyes, willing himself to find the trancelike state that always preceded sleep for him. At last it found him, relaxing him, slowing down his thoughts. Drifting away steadily.

His last waking thought was of Valerie Brigh-ton. A pretty woman. A confident woman. A smart woman with a great deal of self-control. A dedicated woman, especially to her family.

But attractive. Sexy. That image of her almost shocked him awake.

A White woman. Hell, he knew better than that. His one foray into that kind of relationship, many years ago, had made him wise to the reality of this world.

But he sank into dreams anyway, too many of them about Valerie Brighton.

VALERIE ENTERED THE Chamberlain house to find May stretched out on the couch. A new liaison officer occupied the chair across from her. She offered a smile to Valerie but didn't speak. Her name badge said she was Deputy Benton.

May's sleep was less restless than last night, probably because she was too exhausted to toss and turn. Maybe because pleasanter dreams tried to protect her for a little while.

The revolving friends were gone, of course. Much as they wanted to support May, they had husbands, children, household tasks such as making dinner that couldn't be ignored indefinitely. All those things that May now lacked.

Valerie debated only a second or two. Bed or coffee? She opted for the coffee, reluctant to sleep without mentally going over the day's interviews.

Not a bad word anywhere about May or Chet? That seemed so unlikely that she tried to remember more closely. Had anyone seemed evasive? As if they might be lying?

But the day had managed to turn into a blur, and all she had was a small notebook tucked into the pocket of her suit jacket. She studied it as the coffee brewed, wondering if she'd scribbled something there, something that had caught her attention or made her uneasy.

She finally slapped it shut and got her coffee. She carried an extra mug out to Benton, who nodded gratefully, then returned to the kitchen. At least this room hadn't given over entirely to black, chrome and stainless steel. That was probably next on the list.

She wondered vaguely whose idea the decor had been. May's? Chet's? Or both of them? The rest of the house looked like something pulled out of a magazine. It wasn't as if Valerie hadn't seen all this on earlier visits, but she'd never thought about it before.

But even the kitchen was on its way to coldness. A stainless-steel refrigerator. A black and stainless-steel induction stove. A black dishwasher.

Amazing that the counters hadn't been turned white or metal. They still gleamed with blue tiles left from times past.

For all its elegance, this home felt almost monastic.

Why?

And what did it matter?

Only Lizzie's room defied the rest of the house, with pale pink walls, dashes of bright color from toys, bedding a patchwork of red, blue, green and white diamonds. An island of color.

She couldn't help wondering if May and Chet's relationship had started cooling well before their divorce, maybe before Lizzie's arrival. It might have. How would she have known?

At last she gave in to her body. She switched the coffee off and headed for bed.

As she rested her head on the pillow, she thought of Guy Redwing. He seemed capable enough. Steady enough. And he'd made her wonder.

How much unknowing bigotry did she harbor?

Chapter Five

Day three. Too long.

Oh, God, Valerie thought as she showered and dressed for the new day. This time she chose jeans and a warm blue sweater over her preferred suits. She hadn't been blind to the way people looked at her.

May was awake, looking miserable as hell, staring at the coffee table where someone had set a pastry before her, ignoring a cup of coffee.

Valerie pulled one of the chairs near the couch where her sister seemed to have planted herself. The liaison officer remained, looking sleepy. Soon the friends would start their daily rotation.

Valerie reached to hug May. "You hanging in there, sis?"

"What else can I do?" May's voice sounded wobbly. Then her blue eyes, so like her sister's, met Valerie's.

"We're running out of hope, aren't we?"

Forty-eight hours, so crucial, had passed. But Valerie wasn't about to say so. "Of course not," she replied firmly.

"You'll keep looking for her? Please?"

"I wouldn't consider anything else." She gently pushed the pastry May's way. "Come on. You won't be much good to anyone if you starve yourself to death. Heck, you won't even be able to hold Lizzie when we find her."

May's eyes closed briefly. "Please, God," she whispered. Then she reached for the pastry and spoke listlessly. "Want some?"

"I'm going to grab something quick at Maude's. Meet up with Guy." She reached out to squeeze May's hand.

May spoke again. "I'm glad you're on the case."

So was Valerie. She'd have gone stark, staring mad if she'd had to sit on her hands. "Where's Chet?"

"He called. He should be here soon."

"Good." Maybe. Something had torn these two apart. Maybe something more than May had ever mentioned.

With too many questions zinging around inside her head, Valerie made her way to the diner to find Guy. He'd taken a booth near the front window, a view on another cloudless day and a street that was growing busy.

He nodded to her when she sat across from him. He'd been nursing coffee from an insulated carafe that Valerie didn't remember from years ago when she'd visited Maude's. She touched it.

"New?" she asked.

"Quite recent. I heard it was Mavis's idea."

"Wouldn't have been Maude's for certain."

Guy offered a faint smile. "I'm going to have breakfast and so should you."

She didn't need the reminder and felt a brief spurt of irritation. God, another man, another member of the patriarchy that didn't think a woman could take care of herself. Then her irritation passed. Maybe she was being unfair. Yet again.

Eggs, rye toast, bacon. Calories. Cholesterol. Any other time she might have shuddered at her choices.

While they waited, Guy brought the conversation back to the kidnapping. "Did you catch anything yesterday when we talked to people?"

She shook her head. "Nothing I bothered to note."

"Then maybe we need to repeat the interviews, look for any discrepancy."

The next step to be sure, although whether it worked on this kind of crime she didn't know. It couldn't hurt though when they had no leads. "There's got to be something somewhere. What good would it do for a stranger to take a child so young?"

"Beats me. This whole thing stinks to high heaven."

Mavis banged her plate down in front of her. At least that hadn't changed in all these years. She'd sometimes wondered how Maude and her daughter managed to do that without breaking a whole bunch of crockery. The bang, however, seemed more like an announcement.

Stinks to high heaven. She knew where Guy's thoughts were turning and everything within her rebelled. Neither Chet nor May could possibly have disappeared their daughter. Nor did either of them have any reason to, not as firmly rooted as they were in this town. Where could they possibly hide a child? What good would it do either of them? The same questions kept roiling in her, like a rat on a wheel.

The thought that occurred to her next made a cold chill run down her spine, a vision of Lizzie buried in a shallow grave somewhere. She'd thought of that, maybe even mentioned it to Guy, but now it struck her forcefully and tried to consume her with sickening terror.

Could there be that much animosity between May and Chet? Could either of them hate that little girl so much? Could anyone?

She nearly pushed her plate aside as her stomach churned. "Guy, I can't think they..." She trailed off, unable to voice her own thoughts.

"We're police officers," he reminded her. "We have to think of *everything*."

He was right. She couldn't dispute that. No police officer could.

She managed to eat. It wasn't an option.

When they were almost finished with breakfast, Guy spoke again. "I want to take a closer look at Chet."

She pushed her plate aside, hating the direction all this would take her. "Why?"

"Because he didn't get joint custody. Because just a few days before Lizzie disappeared they had a disagreement about whether he could just drop in. You heard what May said."

"But is that enough?"

"Maybe not. We have to look more closely. Something tore that marriage apart. Do you really think it was his work hours?"

She'd begun wondering about that herself. She felt a great deal of liking for Chet but she didn't know him very well. Nor was it likely that May would have told her everything about her decision to file for divorce. Some secrets were better kept for any number of reasons.

Grief and fear slammed her again and she turned quickly away to look out the window once more. She'd already learned that Guy was an astute observer of facial expressions. She didn't want him to read her face right now.

And once again she hated the growing bustle of people outside. Normal lives untouched by a tragedy of this magnitude. The whole damn world should have frozen in its tracks.

GUY HAD WATCHED the flow of emotions across Valerie's face. He wondered if she had any idea how much she betrayed, yet she could become totally impassive on the job. How many times a day did she have to lock away all her emotions in order to be a detective? As many as he did?

Even here in this small town being a cop could get incredibly ugly. For all this was a friendly place where neighbors helped each other out, it was still full of human beings. And human beings could get downright horrible. Some of those smiles out there probably hid dark things: hatred, malice, envy, anger. There were even a few longstanding feuds, but these days they played out mostly in court, unlike past times when they might be settled with guns. Yet the surface around here remained tranquil and pleasant. Most of the time.

Then there was the grapevine. Gossip was a popular activity in these parts. A way to fill some empty hours and maybe play a quiet game of one-upmanship. Like the game of telephone, however, stories stretched and changed along the way. It was usually harmless, but occasionally that grapevine would get clogged with maliciousness and outright lies. One thing was for sure—it was never silent.

But on this matter, at least, the gossip had gone still. Which was interesting in and of itself. By now someone should have started a story about May or Chet. Some ugly tidbit that would grow as it spread. Maybe some little fact that got twisted. Maybe a fully made-up story.

But nothing.

That alone disturbed him. He had no doubt that Gage was right about it. His wife, Emmaline, was plugged into everything in the area. As the head librarian and daughter of a founding family, the Conards, she had deep enough roots to be in touch with it all. She'd know if there were any whispers about the Chamberlains.

The lack of whispers might be speaking loudly. Did it mean no one harbored any ill will against the family? Or did it mean that for once nobody wanted to stir up any kind of trouble because a missing child was involved?

If anyone knew anything that might be helpful but didn't want to say it to anyone else, that would hinder the investigation.

Valerie returned her attention to him. "Have the search parties quit?"

"Not yet. The number of searchers has diminished, though."

"I'd expect that." She frowned. "We're losing precious time."

"Hour by hour," he agreed. And so far they had no damn way of speeding this up. It twisted his gut into a knot when he looked at the problem that way.

He noticed Valerie had begun to aimlessly fold a paper napkin, creasing it sharply. "What?" he asked. Her nervous habit. She'd done it yesterday.

She looked up. "Huh?"

He pointed to the napkin. "What's troubling you apart from Lizzie's disappearance? Because something obviously is. We're not going to get anywhere if you hold anything back. Did you remember something that bothered you about the interviews we did?"

She shook her head slowly. "No. Not exactly." She bit her lower lip, worrying it. "The cop in me is probably getting too suspicious."

"Maybe. Share it anyway."

She suddenly looked stricken. To his surprise his own heart responded to her distress. God, he didn't need that.

She spoke at last. "What Chet and May both

said about Lizzie crying when she's taken from her mother?"

"Yeah? The baby monitor had been shut down."

Valerie shook her head slightly, and her eyes reddened just a bit. "May should have heard her cry anyway."

Guy felt gut-punched. It took him nearly a minute to find his voice and when he did he had to clear his throat. "What do you mean?"

"I could be wrong. God, I hope I'm wrong!"

"But?"

"But Lizzie's room is right next to May's. Those walls aren't soundproofed. Lizzie cries loudly. Monitor or no monitor, May would have had to have been drugged not to hear her. Monitors aren't for hearing from the next room but for being somewhere else in the house."

VALERIE FELT SICK enough to vomit. She resumed folding the napkin, trying to focus on that one little bit of clarity. But the detective in her had fully wakened and she couldn't ignore what she had just figured out.

"That means one of two things," she continued, her voice ragged with squelched emotions. "Either May was drugged somehow or someone did something else to get that child out of the house without crying." She shuddered, unable to hold it all in.

"Or…" Guy let the word hang. He knew he wasn't going to state the unspoken part: that May had gotten rid of her own daughter.

Chapter Six

They left Maude's together, climbed without a word into his Suburban and sat in silence for a century or two, or so it felt to Valerie.

Her chest squeezed so tightly that Valerie doubted she would ever breathe again. Her stomach threatened to eject the food she had just eaten, and with the nausea came a cold sweat.

Words finally burst out of her. "May wouldn't hurt her. Absolutely would not! She adores Lizzie."

"She's also a single mom with an ex who seems unable to accept the terms of the custody arrangement. Or maybe she's being unfair to him, given his irregular hours. That bit sounded a little cruel to me."

Valerie hated to agree, but it had struck her that way, too. Did she want to deprive Chet of all contact with his daughter? Was she that angry and bitter? What had brought on that divorce? Something so ugly that May had never told her own sister?

Guy spoke again after a minute or so. "You need to question her about that."

"I know," Valerie answered, her voice thick. "I

know." She stared through the windshield at the offensive, sunny, normal street. "I'm beginning to wish I'd never insisted on getting involved in this."

Guy snorted. "As if you wouldn't have been thinking like a detective anyway even if all you did was sit this out with May. You're doing it right now even if it's killing you."

Her hands clenched into fists. "I don't know if I can do this, Guy."

"No one else can."

His words dropped into her like hot lava bombs. He was right.

GUY LEFT VALERIE at May's house. She stood on the sidewalk, looking up at the large brick house, feeling almost crushed under the weight of what she needed to do.

More anguish, fear and guilt than she could imagine lay inside that house, a lurking beast. No one, not even Aunt Valerie, could possibly experience the depth of pain that May was feeling.

Now she needed to enter that house in a way that would only make May feel worse. Valerie hated herself.

But it had to be done. Squaring her shoulders, seeking the stability and detachment that had carried her through some truly upsetting cases, she headed for the door. She felt like a high-wire walker with the gaping Grand Canyon beneath her. A misstep might hurt May, it might permanently damage their relationship, and she might fall to an internal death all her own.

God, that was her beloved sister in there. Friends all their lives. The best of buddies, sharing everything.

But maybe something hadn't been shared this time. Something that might help find Lizzie.

Or something that would damn her sister or Chet to eternal fire. She couldn't believe it. She didn't *want* to believe it, but for the next while she *had* to force herself to believe it was possible. Butterflies in the pit of her stomach fluttered so wildly it felt as if they were locked in some kind of battle.

When she entered the house, she found May all alone. Her sister had curled up on the couch and was staring blindly into space.

"May? Where'd everyone go?"

May stirred only slightly. "I told them to leave," she answered dully.

"Why?"

May's voice rose and she sat up. "Because that damn cop was useless. She was sitting there by the hour with nothing to report. Because I can't stand another person trying to tell me it'll be all right."

Valerie shut up, letting her rant, awash in pain for her sister.

"Because," May continued, "I'll scream if one more person offers me tea or coffee or pastry or some sloppy casserole. Because I want to scream every time someone tells me I need to eat something! I'm living in hell and I can't stand anyone telling me that it's going to be okay."

May drew a shuddery breath. "It's not going to be okay. It's not. My baby's out there somewhere, all alone. Frightened. Maybe being mistreated. Maybe *dead*! And no one's helping. No one!"

Then May dissolved into wracking sobs, sobs that threatened to tear her apart. Valerie eased down onto the sofa beside her and wrapped her arms around May, holding her tightly, letting the storm tear at her sister.

Helpless. God, she was so damn helpless and useless. And now she needed to ask questions, awful questions, questions that might tear May apart more. She squeezed her eyes shut, trying to steel herself from the minutes ahead.

When May's sobs began to ease because of fatigue, and she started to sag, Valerie asked quietly, "Where's Chet?"

"Where he always is," May answered wearily. "With some patient who matters more than I do."

So no time with Chet was better than some time with Chet? But hadn't that been the reason for the divorce in the first place?

She stroked her sister's hair. "But he went out with the search parties."

May's voice strengthened, laced with fury. "Big deal. He took a week off when Lizzie was born. One lousy week. His partner couldn't handle the patient load alone. She has a *family* to get home to. Chet covered evenings and nights for her all the time. But not for *his* family. So *I* had to handle it all alone. God, the people in this county must be breeding like rabbits!"

"Did you have a problem with that before Lizzie was born?" Valerie couldn't remember any complaints before then.

May sniffled, drew back and grabbed a tissue from the nearby box to dab at her eyes. "I didn't notice it as much. I had my teaching job. I was bringing home my work all the time. I was *busy.*"

Valerie drew a breath. "So Lizzie changed all that."

"Of course she did. It's different with a baby. I stopped working because I needed to take care of her and I didn't want to be sending her to day care five days a week. I wanted to take care of my own baby, not let someone else do it."

Valerie nodded, taking it all in, feeling May's words pierce her like knives. She steadied herself with a deep breath. She couldn't afford to give in to her own anguish. *Not now.*

May spoke again. "At first it wasn't so bad. I was walking on air. Then it changed."

"How so?"

May didn't answer for a while, then: "I started to feel bad. Resentful. Dulled by it all. Chet said it was postpartum depression. He wanted to give me a pill for it. A pill! Like that would change anything about the situation. I was basically locked up in this house with an infinite sea of diapers and a kid who needed me all the damn time. Sure, friends would stop by, but conversation gets pretty dull when all you have to talk about is diapers and babies. And it left me feeling left out as they shared all *their* stories of the day."

Valerie took her sister's hand and held it snugly, stating the obvious. "I can't say I understand how it was for you."

May turned her head, looking at Valerie from wet eyes. "I loved Lizzie all the time, though. You need to understand. No matter how miserable I was feeling, I always loved her. I *do* love her."

"Of course." Valerie had begun to feel she was swimming in unfamiliar waters and couldn't find her footing. She didn't know how to reach out. She'd never had to reach out to anyone in this state of turmoil. She was also getting a better idea of what May had been going through.

May wiped her nose with the tissue. "Chet was here when he had the time, just like always. But I started to feel he wanted to get away from me. Like he was working more than usual just to escape my moods, to escape all the work involved. Maybe that wasn't fair, but I began to believe it. Then came the colic."

Valerie waited. She wanted May to tell the story her own way.

"Do you know anything about colic? It can go on for months. There's no help for it. It lasts three or four hours at a time, usually, and you feel so damn helpless walking a screaming child you can't help. Night after night. It seemed like it would go on forever."

"And Chet?"

"He helped when he was here," she said fairly. "But he wasn't here very much. An awful lot of babies were being born during the nights. Then there were his office hours." She sniffled again. "Do you think he was running away? Or having an affair?"

Valerie felt shock all the way to her toes. Chet having an affair? That had never entered her head. He didn't seem like the type. "Only Chet can answer that question," she answered carefully.

"Like he ever would. I demanded to know and he denied it all. Work was his everlasting excuse. If I was going to have to deal with it all alone, so be it. I divorced him. The only thing he fought me about was custody."

"How did *you* feel about the divorce?"

"Free." May wiped her eyes again and spoke fiercely. "He was no longer a problem for me. Whatever his reasons he was gone and, without worrying about what was going on with him, I started to enjoy Lizzie even more."

May fell silent for a while, her tears dried up, her breaths growing calmer. When she spoke again, she said, "He was rejecting me so I rejected him."

EVENTUALLY MAY AGREED to eat something, to drink some coffee. Valerie found the refrigerator overflowing with well-meaning gifts of food. Plenty to choose from. Given May's state her sister needed some hefty fuel to keep herself going, so Valerie chose some sweet, fatty pastries to go with the coffee. She carried plates and mugs for them both and placed them on the coffee table. This time May reached for the pastry without being prodded.

But Valerie had gotten the clearer picture she'd needed. Roses hadn't turned to ashes because anything had changed except May. She faced it squarely. May said she loved Lizzie, had never stopped loving her, but was that true?

Given the situation and how May had come to feel about Chet, fairly or unfairly, the divorce made sense. She wondered about Chet's version of events and whether she could get him to talk about it.

When May ate half the pastry and appeared inclined to eat no more, Valerie asked gently, "Your life changed drastically with Lizzie but Chet's didn't."

"Exactly. That's it exactly. Plus I didn't feel I could trust him anymore."

It all made sense, Valerie thought as she watched May wipe her fingers and mouth on a napkin.

But she was haunted by a memory. A woman she'd known years back had commented on a news story about a mother who'd killed her own son. *There but for the Grace of God*, she'd said.

Valerie had asked her what she'd meant.

The friend had looked at her and replied, *You have no idea how far up the wall a kid can drive you, especially as they get older. I once got so angry, worn out and sick of the constant arguments that I had a vision of banging my son's head against the wall. It shocked the hell out of me.*

Then the woman had added, *The only difference*

*between her and me is that one split second of clear
thought.*

Well, Valerie had seen plenty of that during her
years with the police. When that one split second
of clear thought never came it resulted in horrific
crimes. The pleas—*I didn't mean to do it.* Too late.

May could have missed that instant of clear
thought. Some people did.

Valerie again felt sick enough to throw up.

ON THE OFF CHANCE that someone they'd interviewed
the preceding day might have remembered something, Guy went back to question some of the people. Besides, while he'd thought Valerie's presence
might loosen tongues, her being May's sister, she
might just as well have silenced people who didn't
want to criticize May in front of her sister. But he'd
had that thought before and all that mattered was
that it propelled him.

He hoped he wasn't wasting valuable time, but
what other leads did he have?

Besides, Valerie was doing the hard part, talking
to her sister. He didn't envy her that task at all. Much
as he didn't want to give the woman any props, he
had to about this.

His initial impression of her was changing. He
no longer saw her as an interloper who looked down
on him. She seemed determined to be professional.
Neither had he noticed anything else that might in-
dicate she was a bigot.

Although a lot of people could succeed in concealing bigotry when it suited them, at least for a while.

He shook his head at himself as he worked his way through the interviews again, briefer this time because he only needed to know one thing: if anyone had heard anything about enemies of the Chamberlains or something unflattering about either of them. He gently prodded them to think more closely.

He got no further than he and Valerie had the day before, which frustrated him no end. There was nobody on this planet who didn't have an enemy somewhere. The Chamberlains weren't saints. No one was, at least among the living.

He stopped by the command post again and found Connie Parish back on duty. The search teams had thinned out and the hope that they'd find the child anywhere in the vicinity had just about died.

Which might be a good thing, he thought as he returned to the Chamberlain house. If Lizzie had been kidnapped—and it was beginning to look as if she had—then she might still be alive. It just widened the search area, though only God knew by how many miles.

Lizzie's photo and description had gone out on the extended Amber Alert Gage had issued that morning. Prior to that, however, there'd been absolutely no evidence that the child might have been taken. Now every policeman in a four-state area was on the lookout. So were caring members of the public.

But nothing yet.

Guy pulled over to the side of the street, needing

to gather himself before seeing Valerie or her sister. Life had hardened him in a lot of ways, but he wasn't hardened to the plight of any child.

This case had pierced his heart.

Chapter Seven

Chet Chamberlain had moved into a small house in a subdivision nearer to the hospital. The subdivision, so unlike much of the rest of Conard City, had been built because of the GI Bill after the Second World War. The houses were aging and basically graceless, but most had been maintained well enough over the years.

They were also small houses. Conard City didn't boast a huge number of large ones, although during boom days the wealthier citizens had constructed mansions along Front Street and nearby. Or at least mansions compared to everything else around here, Chet thought.

Not that he truly cared. The small place he lived in now was big enough for him. Two bedrooms, one of them an office for him, a basic kitchen and living area. It was enough room, and a place where he didn't spend much time.

It also didn't hold memories and dreams, unlike the big house he had deeded over to May. *That* place had once been full of dreams that he and May had shared. Now it held only pain for him. He wondered if May felt the same pain but doubted it. She'd been the one who had demanded a divorce.

The situation with Lizzie was eating him alive. The house he hunkered down in no longer felt like a hidey-hole. When he walked in there now, he could only hear Lizzie's laugh, hear the sound of her running feet. He kept turning, expecting to see her. He wondered if May felt the same way in that big house, or if the sea of agony had swamped her.

It hadn't quite swamped him yet, but he was holding it at bay by diving into his work. He couldn't think of one damn useful thing to do about his daughter, and he couldn't offer comfort to May. There was no comfort to be offered, not when the whole thing was tearing him to pieces, too—not when she'd thrown him out. He wondered briefly if she knew he felt the same fear and worry she did, then cast the stupid question aside. Of course she did.

He'd been cut off and with the severing of that tie he was left alone in a situation that made him want to rend the very heavens. Why would May even think about what *he* was feeling?

He had just come back from the hospital and poured himself a finger of whiskey, shutting his ears to the sounds of Lizzie, already imprinted on this place from her too-short visits. He couldn't bear to think of where she might be now, how she was.

It was almost a relief when Valerie knocked on his door and told him she needed to talk with him. He let her in, asking immediately if there was any news.

Hope's tendrils tightened around his heart along with the agony that wouldn't quit.

Val shook her head. "I'm sorry, not a word. But I need to talk with you, Chet. If you can stand it."

Chet waved her to a chair but remained standing himself, glass in hand. "Want a drink?"

Val shook her head. "This wouldn't be a good time."

"No, it's not," he agreed, looking at the whiskey. "But it's all I have right now." Unable to hold still, he paced the small living room with its sofa, recliner and TV. "You've come to play detective, I suppose."

He heard her sigh and finally looked at her. Really looked at her. "What did I say?"

She gave him a small shake of her head. "*Detective* isn't something I play at."

"Oh, for God's sake, Val, you know I didn't mean it that way. What's wrong with you?"

"Only the same thing that's wrong for all of us right now."

He saw her eyes redden and realized Lizzie's disappearance was hurting her almost as much as it was hurting May and himself. A new ache slipped through him as he wondered why he hadn't considered Val's feelings in all of this. Maybe because she always seemed so self-possessed? So confident? Or maybe he wasn't as empathetic as he believed?

"I'm sorry," he said after another swig of his whiskey. "I'm a mess. I'd claw something to death if I could. Scream. Chew nails. Shoot myself."

That got her full attention. "Shoot yourself? Why?"

"Because this has to be my fault somehow! Ask May, everything's my fault!" His voice had risen and he fought to force himself back into the zone where he could treat patients who were in the worst of crises. Patients who needed him to remain calm no matter what. It wasn't easy in this situation. Not that it ever was, but Lizzie being gone? That was whole orders of magnitude worse than anything he'd ever faced.

"You think May's blaming you?" She tilted her head, then rose and headed for the small table where the liquor bottle sat along with a few highball glasses. "She's not blaming you," she told him as she poured a small amount of whiskey for herself.

"If she isn't, she will eventually," he answered, bitterness replacing everything else inside him. "God, it got to the point where I couldn't do a damn thing right. May turned into someone I could hardly recognize. But I'd have waited it out, Val. She would have gotten past it all. Despite what she might say, I wasn't the one who changed."

Holding her glass, Val perched on the edge of the recliner. "I heard May's side of the divorce, but what about yours?"

He glared at her and drained his glass. "Are you blaming me for this?"

"I'm not blaming anyone," she said gently. "I just want to understand."

"Understand what? I already told you. May *changed*."

"Okay. How did you feel when she told you she didn't want you dropping in to see Lizzie?"

He felt his mouth twist. The detective was here, and her kid gloves would come off if necessary. "It made me feel godawful. *She* was the one who argued I shouldn't get joint custody because of my irregular hours. So what am I supposed to do? Stick to a weekend here and there when I might have to run out to work? Leave Lizzie with a babysitter? The babysitter she didn't want me to get?"

Val nodded slowly. "I see your point."

"At least *you* do," he said bitterly. He turned away to look out his front window at the deepening night. Lizzie was out there somewhere. Terror gripped him.

"Tell me, if you can, who might have a grudge against you? Anything that springs to mind."

He continued to stare at the window, and now ice filled him. "A lot of people," he said eventually, his mind springing them up like weeds in a badly kept lawn.

He heard Val move behind him. "Who?" she asked.

"Dozens of people. Maybe more." Now he turned to face her, the ice in his veins hardening. "Do you have any idea why obstetricians and gynecologists carry the most expensive malpractice insurance in the medical field? It's so bad a lot of medical school graduates look for any other area of practice."

"Why is that?"

"Because," he answered harshly, "we get blamed for everything that goes wrong. We get blamed for stillbirths, genetic defects. Mother Nature doesn't get the blame even though we don't cause the problem. No, *we* get sued. How the hell am I to blame for Down syndrome or cystic fibrosis? Or any of a million things that can go wrong with a fetus? How can we be blamed if a mother doesn't take her prenatal vitamins and has a child with spina bifida? You want the whole list?"

"That's not necessary," she said quietly. "I'm sorry, Chet. It shouldn't be that way."

"No, it shouldn't, but insurance companies find it cheaper to settle a lawsuit than to fight it. So there you have it."

He poured himself another whiskey.

Valerie spoke again. "Think about it, Chet. Please. Anyone you can think of who might want to hurt you through Lizzie. We need all the help we can get, okay?"

"I'll try. As if I can focus on anything except Lizzie."

"Can you go through your records and see if anyone stands out? That might be a real help in this search."

"Okay." He gritted his teeth. "Okay. I'll look. I'll get some medical people to help looking at the files to speed it up." His face sagged. "It won't help."

Now her voice developed an edge. "Why not?"

The detective was here, he reminded himself. Not the Val he knew as a fun sister-in-law.

"HIPAA," he finally answered savagely. "Patients have a right to privacy under federal law. I can't tell you *anything*!"

He stared down at the glass in his hand, then hurled it across the room at the wall, where it shattered into pieces, just like his heart.

"She's my baby," he said as the tsunami washed over him again. *"She's my baby."*

Guy Redwing waited outside in his official Suburban. Valerie felt almost weak as she walked toward his car, her legs shaking as if they could no longer support her. He climbed out and met her halfway.

"Valerie?" he asked.

"It's not him," she said brokenly, then did something she hadn't done in her entire career. She collapsed against him, tears pouring out of her, grateful when his strong arms wrapped around her and held her close. She needed him desperately.

Guy helped her into his vehicle, then drove away from Chet's place, not sure what to do. The strong woman in the passenger seat was breaking down, understandably, but the situation was awkward beyond belief. She might well hate him for seeing her weakness. He'd already figured out that she was a woman who hated to show weakness. Powerful. Strong. Capable. That's the image she projected and most likely the person she was.

Until this. He shook his head a little as he drove aimlessly. This would kill just about anyone, he thought. Not only worrying about her niece and her sister but needing to be a detective through it all. He couldn't imagine.

But he didn't need to imagine it. It was happening in the seat right beside him. When the storm passed, she was probably going to hate him for seeing her like this. Hate herself.

So what now? How could he shelter her without making her feel worse? Damned if he had any idea.

"Want to go back to May's?" he asked when she seemed calmer.

Her voice was thick. "No! Not yet. I don't think I've ever felt so helpless in my life, Guy. I'm not ready to prop up my sister, not yet."

He thought of Chet Chamberlain. "Maybe someone else should do a little of the propping. Like Chet."

"He seems to be convinced she doesn't want him around. That she's going to start blaming him for whatever has happened to Lizzie."

His interest perked but he let it slide for now. He didn't think pushing her was going to be any help to her just then. Let it rest until she was ready to talk about it.

"How about I pick up something at Maude's? Then we can go to my place for a bit. Just to give you a break."

"I shouldn't need a break. I'm just doing my damn job."

"Right," he said sarcastically. "Under any other circumstances, I'd probably agree with you."

He didn't wait for her to come up with any more

objections. He drove to Maude's, grabbed some steak sandwiches and salad, and returned to his vehicle with a couple of bags. Valerie sat quietly, staring out the passenger window. He doubted she was seeing anything that wasn't inside her.

Chapter Eight

Over all these years in Conard County, Guy had rented an apartment in the complex that had been built so long ago by a short-lived semiconductor plant, but was now used primarily for student housing. He'd done little to improve it, just a recliner and a second-hand dinette set. A single wall-hanging of a rug his mother had woven. A bed, of course.

And on the one battered side table a photo of his immediate family. A reminder of those he loved, some who barely spoke to him since he'd put on a badge.

He placed their boxed dinners on a rickety kitchen table, started some coffee, and pulled out a few chipped plates along with some scratched silverware.

He saw his quarters with fresh eyes as he led Valerie inside. It wasn't much.

"I like the blanket," she said. "Beautiful."

"My mother made it."

He felt her gaze on him as he set out the utensils and opened the box. "Grab a seat. The chair will hold you and the table won't collapse."

She looked around the small kitchen, then sat. "You like it like this?"

"It's better than where I lived on the rez."

Her face changed infinitesimally as he put food on the plates, then poured two mugs of coffee. At least the cups weren't chipped.

She took a small bite of the sandwich. "These are still as good as they used to be."

"As reliable as Maude."

When she swallowed a second mouthful, she asked, "Was your childhood awful?"

"No. The winters could be hard, though, when we couldn't pay for enough heating oil. But by and large it was good. Plenty of loving family and friends."

She hesitated visibly. "I thought the government built houses on the reservation."

"If you can call boxes with poor insulation and dirt floors houses."

"God, Guy!"

He finished his sandwich and started on the salad before he spoke again. "Try finding a job when you're a redskin."

"But…" She bit her lip. "Isn't that an awful word?"

"Just the one I heard a thousand times. We all got labeled drunks and layabouts. Indigent instead of Indigenous. Especially hard for the women."

She pushed her salad around her plate. "How so?"

"Have you ever heard of MMIW? Missing and Murdered Indigenous Women?"

She pushed the salad aside and looked at him from a pale face. "Tell me."

He waved a hand. "When Indigenous women turn up missing or murdered, the cops barely investigate. For rapes it's even worse."

She leaned back and drew a shaky breath. "I don't have words. Is that why you became a cop?"

"Yeah. That's it. I swore I was going to change things in my small part of the world. Some of my friends and family don't get it. They think I went over to the dark side."

"God! How do you stand it?"

"Because I have to."

Telling her all this had only roiled up feelings he'd spent years burying. That clawing rage filled him once again. To distract himself from it, he went to get them more coffee.

She looked at the mug. "I could do with a drink."

"Sorry, I don't touch alcohol."

Her expression filled with sorrow. "Because of the labels?"

"Because Indigenous people are genetically prone to alcohol addiction."

She drew a sharp breath. "But how…"

He shook his head. "The Aztecs knew it. They had rules about it. Only small children and the elderly and sick could drink alcoholic beverages. The rest of the time it was off-limits. Anyway, I hear they found the genetic reason. I don't know for sure. But I've seen enough of my people succumb. Never a drop for me."

He sat again. "You wouldn't believe the number of liquor stores around the edges of a reservation.

Even though it's not allowed on the rez, plenty of people go off the rez to buy it. The Whites love it."

His hands clenched. "We try to protect ourselves and get sabotaged. The Navajo Nation is better about it. They'll arrest anyone, Whites included, if they're found with alcohol on the rez. Not everyone has a big enough police force to stop it. That costs money, which a lot of nations don't have. What does it matter anyway if some of the cops are addicted, too? Why should they care? Anyway, it gives them a good excuse to crack down on drunken Indians."

"I never thought about it," she admitted. "Never."

"Why would you? Easier to think of us as drunks."

She shook her head, falling silent. Then, "Is that why you wear your uniform instead of plainclothes?"

"Believe it. Like I said, it greases the wheels. That uniform puts me in a special category. Folks might not like it when I'm the responding officer, but they don't hassle me. Not often, anyway."

"I can't imagine, Guy. I just can't imagine."

"You don't need to." Shoving his anger back down into his box of private furies, he forced himself to relax. "I'm lucky I got the job here. To *be* here. Micah Parish paved the way a long time ago. Then there's the vet. Mike Windwalker. A few little steps, among others, toward acceptance."

Once again she fell silent.

Eventually he spoke. "I shouldn't have dumped all that on you. You've got enough on your plate right now."

"I'm glad you told me. There's so much I don't

understand. Now I'll know to be on the lookout for this crap."

Nevertheless, he felt like a jerk for letting all of that ugliness out, and worse for speaking of it to Valerie. No way to make amends for it. He'd spewed it and now he had to live with it. The way he always lived with the consequences of his actions.

But he moved away quickly from his own problems and back to hers. More important right now. "So you really think Chet couldn't have had anything to do with this?"

"Not directly." Now she reached for her cooling coffee and downed half of it.

"Need some water?" Guy asked. "You look thirsty."

"Please."

He went to the fridge and pulled out a bottle. "Mind drinking it like this or do you want a glass?"

She gave him a faint half smile. "I'm not a hothouse flower. Gimme that bottle."

In spite of himself, he nearly smiled as he passed her the bottle. She drank half of it before setting it aside.

But now it was time to deal with the *other* difficulty. He repeated the question. "You said you think Chet had nothing to do with Lizzie's disappearance?"

"I don't. I don't think May did either. I listened to them, Guy. I couldn't mistake their pain, and I believed what they both said. There's a wrinkle, though."

He stiffened, expecting her to give him bad news. "What?"

"I asked Chet to check his records for anyone who might bear a grudge. He said he would, but it wouldn't do any good. HIPAA. He can't reveal any personal health information under federal law."

"Damn it!" He drummed his fingers on the table, a moderate reaction to the surge of fresh anger he felt. Hell, he hated this case. He hated what it was doing to so many people. He hated that every twist and turn took them nowhere. He hated that a child was at risk.

She spoke. "I feel the same. I don't know what kind of trouble Chet might get into if he flouts that law. Federal penalties, certainly."

"Penalties he might not care about if he develops a strong opinion about who might be involved."

She drew another deep breath. "Maybe."

"That's a thin thread to cling to." He rose, pacing every inch of this tiny apartment. "There's got to be something somewhere. I know some people disappear into thin air, but a small child? A kid who's hardly more than an infant?"

"Damn it, Guy, I don't even want to think about how that could happen!"

He stopped pacing. "I'm sorry."

Finally, she shook her head. "We're cops. We've got to think about it."

Horror filled him when she spoke the dreaded words.

"Does this county have any cadaver dogs?"

Chapter Nine

"No," he answered heavily. "No. Some trackers but not that. And the K-9s couldn't even pick up a scent around the house."

Tears began to pour down Valerie's face. "We've got to."

"I'll find one. Some department in this state must have one. Or maybe more. But are you sure you want to do this? It's basically giving up hope."

"You think I don't know that?" She jumped up, hugging herself, her tears growing more copious. "But there has to be a resolution of some kind. This can't go on forever!"

That she would even think of a cadaver dog told him how deeply she had sunk into the horror of this situation. Almost beyond rescue. Or maybe far beyond it unless they found Lizzie alive.

She turned toward him, and without thinking about it, he wrapped her in his arms again, wishing he could be a bulwark rather than merely a companion as she walked through this fire.

He had no words to offer, no clues to help the situation, nothing but a pair of arms to let her know he cared, that he was there for her. Other than that, he was totally useless.

He'd solved many cases over his career, but never had he wanted more to solve one. To bring relief to Valerie and her family. Helpless, he offered all that he could.

WITHIN GUY'S EMBRACE, Valerie felt herself softening. The tightly coiled spring inside her eased, letting her go until she relaxed deep within.

But she felt ashamed and humiliated by her uncharacteristic reaction, by revealing herself as weak and worn out. She'd had some tough times as a cop; she carried hideous memories that often disturbed her sleep until they faded into an ugly background. But never before had she broken down.

She *didn't* break down. Never had. Yet here she was, clinging to a man as if he were a lifeline. She disgusted herself.

Yet she couldn't move away. She'd found a haven and didn't want to leave it. When he loosened his hug just a bit, a sense of panic filled her, but then in his gentler embrace he began to rub his hands over her back. Soothing her. Calming her even more.

"Like a horse," she said suddenly, her voice raw.

"Huh?"

"You're soothing me like a horse."

A snort escaped him. "Cripes, Valerie, I've never hugged a horse in my life."

She tilted her head in order to see his chiseled face. "Are you sure?"

He shook his head slowly. "I'm sure. And I've been around plenty of horses. Damn, Valerie, you don't remind me of a horse at all."

"I hope not." Then she forced herself to back away, dashing away those embarrassing tears on the sleeve of her sweater. As soon as she did, the pain started to return. She could get through this, though. On her *own* two feet, not his. She *had* to or she'd lose her sense of self, her confidence in her ability to take it all on the chin.

With each step she took away from him she felt as if she were ripping her skin off, returning to the raw nerve ending she seemed to have become. She resumed her seat at the rickety table.

"Sorry about that," she managed to say. But she wasn't, not really. A part of her, disgusting as it was, had found a few minutes of calm in the hurricane of horror that buffeted her. Had, perhaps, given her a clearer mind.

Guy stared at her for a couple of minutes, then went to the wall phone to punch in a number. "Gage? Sorry to disturb your evening, but Valerie and I want you to find a cadaver dog. Maybe a team of them."

Once again Valerie tightened like a coiled spring. All of it was back, cloaking her like wet, dead leaves.

"Yeah. Thanks." Guy hung up. "Gage knows of a private group. He'll get them."

She whispered, "I can't believe I asked for that."

"You walk down every avenue you have on a case.

You know that. So we'll walk down this road and God willing these dogs won't find any more than the K-9s did." He sat across from her, studying her as if waiting for another emotional outburst.

She wouldn't give it to him. Wouldn't feel guilty about another one. With difficulty, she forced herself back to her detective self.

"I can't believe the K-9s didn't find anything at all."

"Me neither. You'd have expected them to catch Lizzie's scent outside the house. Or the scent of someone else who'd been in her bedroom with her. Nothing."

"How is that possible?" But she knew it was possible. And that was the only reason she'd asked for a cadaver dog.

She jumped up, pacing as Guy had such a short while ago, although she felt as if she'd climbed ten mountains inside herself since then. Now she simply couldn't hold still.

"My sister," she said. "My former brother-in-law. Will I ever be able to see them the same way again? All this suspicion. It stains things forever. May sure won't see me the same way again. Ever."

"You can't know that."

She turned on him, feeling her face twist. "Really? The minute those cadaver dogs show up, she's going to know exactly what we've been thinking about. She's going to *know*. Our relationship will never recover."

"If she gets closure…"

"That's an overused pop psychology word. Closure? How can there be any real closure to something that will cause you pain for the rest of your life? Knowing isn't really enough. Like in a book, it's the hook at the end of a chapter to pull you forward. But it doesn't pull you out of the story. You don't get any closure to the book until you read the last sentence. Until you finish your life."

Guy shook his head. "That's bleak."

"It's also true. Tell me I'm wrong."

Clearly he couldn't. His usually impassive face revealed little, but she could still sense hidden emotions playing across it. She just couldn't read him. That could get frustrating, she realized. It was frustrating right now.

Wrapping her arms around herself again, she resumed pacing. "The hours are passing. The precious forty-eight are gone."

"If it's a kidnapping there might be more hours."

"So where's the ransom note, Guy? Where is it?"

THAT BOTHERED GUY, TOO. There had to be a motive for Lizzie's kidnapping, if that's what it was. So why no note? Why silence?

The first thoughts that occurred to him were so despicable he refused to entertain them. "Maybe somebody just wants a baby."

She froze midstride, then faced him again. "It's happened," she said hoarsely.

"That's why hospitals have such stringent security precautions these days."

She sat with a thud. "You're right."

But how did they trace that one? "We should start searching for someone who suddenly has a child Lizzie's age."

"Maybe so," she answered. "But how? A little kid could be explained away as a niece who'd come to visit. Or as a child from a previous marriage. Or the kidnapper could live in a place isolated enough that no one would see."

"It won't hurt to send out a bulletin. Maybe the Amber Alert isn't enough. Maybe it needs refreshing."

Valerie nodded, hope pricking the agony in her heart. Just a little prick she didn't dare nourish.

Guy continued. "This kidnapper would have to eventually buy something for a kid that age. A toy. Most likely clothes. This kind of kidnapper wants to treat a child as his or her own."

"Wants to enjoy parenthood," Valerie agreed. "That might be enough, but how long will it take?"

"Conard County isn't the only place in Wyoming with a grapevine. I don't know how long it might take, but sooner or later someone is going to notice something. Maybe as a result of the Amber Alert. Or maybe just because they find it suspicious."

She began to rub her upper arms and Guy asked, "You getting chilled? I can turn up the heat."

Valerie shook her head. "I'm a wreck, that's all. Self-comfort, I guess." She dropped her hands.

Not knowing where else to take this, he asked,

"Want some fresh coffee? Or a bed? You can have mine. I can sleep in the recliner."

"I'm not sure I'll ever sleep again. I should go back to May, but I'm still not ready. After the way I questioned her, I don't think she'll be happy with me. Regardless, the state I'm in, I'm not sure I could be supportive enough."

But then she rose.

"Enough. She's probably sitting there all alone. I can't leave her that way just because I'm having a crisis."

Guy rose, too. "I'll take you."

And maybe he'd go inside with her. Handle the tough questions May was bound to ask. Spare Valerie as much as he could.

He'd expected this partnership to be a whole lot different. Instead her grief was welding them into a tight team.

A White woman. Damn it all to hell! Hadn't he learned?

WHEN THEY ARRIVED at May's house, Sheriff Gage Dalton was limping toward the front door. He paused as Guy and Valerie pulled up.

He greeted them with a short nod. "Anything?"

"Ideas," Guy answered. "Nothing we want to discuss in front of May unless it appears it might help her. I'll let Valerie be the judge of that. Otherwise, we'll tell you later."

Gage looked at the house. "I don't like what's happening in there. That poor woman. That poor child.

Lizzie's old enough to be terrified out of her mind. Just let me get my hands on the perp."

"And you'll arrest him," Valerie said. "Or her. Another wrecked life won't help anything."

Gage gave her his half smile. "At least one of us has a clear head."

"Not really," Valerie said. "Hearing you say it, well, I feel the same so I can hand *you* the advice. And remind myself."

Valerie opened the door for them. No knock. May wasn't in sight.

"May?" she called, her heart starting to race. She hoped May hadn't done something stupid.

But then May appeared from the bedroom area. She looked haggard. "I was just sitting in Lizzie's room." In her hand she held a small blanket. "It's all I have left."

Valerie hurried to her and hugged her tightly. "We're working on it, I swear."

"Yeah," May said wearily. She pulled away and dropped onto the couch, holding the blanket to her face. "I can still smell her. But it's not enough!"

"Of course not," Valerie answered, sitting beside her.

May looked past her at Guy and Gage, speaking on a rising note. "Both of you? Bad news?"

"No news," Valerie answered swiftly. "Not yet."

"But when? Oh, God, when?"

"We've got some leads," Guy answered. "We're working on them." He took a chair facing her and after a brief hesitation Gage took the other.

"I may need help getting out of this chair," he remarked absently. Then he turned his attention to May. "We're calling in some extra dogs. Maybe that will help."

Valerie was grateful for the way he phrased it.

"Help how?" May demanded. "Do you know how long she's been out there?"

"We do," Guy answered gently.

"Then she's dead! *Dead!* I can't believe that. I won't believe that!"

"That's not what we're saying," Valerie interjected quickly. "Extra dogs might pick up a scent where the others failed."

May's eyes had grown watery again, but tears didn't fall. She probably didn't have a tear left to shed, Valerie thought. "We're thinking it might be a kidnapping."

May's head jerked. "Your questions weren't about that. I listened."

"Then maybe you didn't hear me quite the right way. I can't promise that's what happened, but we're seriously thinking about it, okay?"

May nodded stiffly and looked at the blanket she was holding so tightly. "Lizzie," she murmured. "Who would steal her? Why?"

Well, those were precisely the right questions, Val thought miserably. Questions without answers like everything else in this disappearance.

Gage spoke. "May, we've got everyone working on this. And not just in Conard County. Everyone wants to find Lizzie. *Everyone.*"

May sighed and sagged, letting her head fall against the back of the sofa. She continued to clutch Lizzie's blanket. "I don't know how much more of this I can take. God help me, I can't stand this."

WITH LITTLE MORE to offer, Valerie followed Gage and Guy out the door.

"Well?" Gage asked. "And *cadaver* dogs?"

"I thought of it," Valerie said, not wanting Guy to take any heat about it.

"*You* did." Gage studied her carefully. "Why?"

"Because it needs to be done. I'm still a cop, much as this mess is tearing me apart."

Gage nodded. "I agree, although I didn't want to say so to you. I contacted a couple of teams and they should be here tomorrow."

Valerie couldn't bring herself to answer. She was having enough trouble dealing with what this might mean.

Guy spoke. "Valerie talked to May and Chet again today. I reinterviewed everyone we'd already spoken to. No dice."

Gage sighed and rubbed his chin. "May and Chet?"

"They didn't do it," Valerie said with conviction. "Neither one of them is playacting. Chet said he'd go back through his medical files to see if there's anyone who might bear a grudge against him, not that it will help. He can't reveal any information. HIPAA."

Gage swore. "Another dead end. I'll have to see if we can't get a warrant to look at any files he consid-

ers possibilities, or even just get names." He paused.
"I'd be damned surprised if we can't get a warrant to
review the files. Okay, that's next on my list."

Valerie felt a tide of relief. More possible leads.
At this point she'd settle for just one.

"Thank you, Gage."

"I wish I could say it was my pleasure but nothing about this is a pleasure. Catch up on your rest,
both of you. You're going to need clear heads tomorrow. I hope we're not all destroyed when those dogs
start searching. I can't bear the thought that Lizzie
isn't still alive and I don't care how far or how long
this takes." He looked at Valerie. "That's a promise."

After Gage left, Valerie turned to Guy. "You
know I can't possibly begin to thank you."

"No need. My job."

"It's more than that and you know it." She looked
down. "It's not normal for me to break down."

"It's not normal that you're investigating a case
involving your niece and your sister. Take it easy
on yourself."

She managed a small smile for him. "Still, I'm
grateful."

They said good-night and Val walked back into
the house, into the hurricane of her sister's grief and
the storm of her own anguish.

FAR OUT ON a ranch, Etta Margolis looked at another
envelope from her ex, Phillip. Why wouldn't he just
leave her alone? He'd sure left her alone in the after-
math of the stillbirth of their child. His ranting, his

anger, most of it had been directed at her because it *had* to be someone's fault.

She knew from listening to her doctor, Chet Chamberlain, that often there was no explanation. Nature made mistakes. Not the mother, not the doctor. Things went wrong with babies at any time during their development. Their son had been one of those mistakes.

But Phillip had been impossible, making her sorrow all the greater with his accusations, refusing to believe that her grief mattered compared to his fury.

She'd almost thrown the envelope in the trash like the first one, but the arrival of a second letter troubled her. They hadn't passed a word in all this time. The letters were so out of character for him that a smidgeon of curiosity awoke in her.

Maybe she should read it, just to see what was going on. If he wanted to get back together she'd write and tell him to shove it. The idea of rejecting him in no uncertain terms gave her a quiver of pleasure, the first she'd felt in a long time.

So she ripped the envelope open and got a huge shock.

Etta, I found a baby for us. She's about the same age our son would have been. Doesn't that make you happy?

She crumpled the note and threw it on the compost like the first one. The man was truly insane. Then she buried the brief note with pitchforkfuls of more compost.

How could he adopt a child? He was a divorced

man with a police record for having beaten Etta, even though she hadn't dared to follow through.

Yeah, Phillip had tipped over the final edge. Putting it from her mind, she turned on the TV.

It was good to be free of Phillip. Maybe the best thing about her life in the last two years. She wasn't going to let him worm his way back in. Miserable and lonely as her life now was, she didn't want him to fill any part of it.

Satisfied with her decision, she put on some sitcom. Even canned laughter sounded good these days. But never the news. Never. She had enough reality to cope with inside herself.

Chapter Ten

Guy returned to his ratty apartment, seeing it through Valerie's eyes, then wondering why he should. It was *his* place, damn it, and it sufficed. Why should he care about her approval?

The fact that he might troubled him.

Then there was his outburst about life as an Indigenous person. Why had he felt the urge to tell her something so personal? It wasn't as if she could help change the reality of it any more than *he* could.

So much for his belief that working inside the system might help his people. Maybe he should just quit and go home apologetically to his family.

But no. Regardless of whether he changed this small bit of the world, the job needed doing and he took a great deal of pride in his work. It satisfied him. It also gave him some control, though not enough. More than he'd had on the rez.

How could he even think of quitting at a time like this anyway? His detachment as a cop was beginning to desert him big-time. As had happened with Valerie, although she had a better excuse than *he* did.

He made some instant cocoa, unable to face another cup of coffee, and headed for his recliner, his mind shifting gears to all the interviews he'd repeated. He still couldn't believe that no one had any unkind words about the Chamberlains. Nobody was *that* good.

There ought to be at least some envy out there. The Chamberlains were relatively well-off for these parts. Big fancy house, new-model cars, maybe even some exotic vacations.

And what about Chet? Had no woman ever made a play for him? A woman whose advances might have been rejected? The same thing went for May, a beautiful woman. Although women with babies were less likely to interest men. Usually.

Had one of them been cheating? Given Chet's apparent hours, he was the likeliest one to have a second relationship, one easy to conceal.

Time to get to Chet's coworkers, to get beyond the teachers, the preschool, and neighbors. So far they'd been too busy to get to that obvious arena.

Tomorrow, he decided. It had waited long enough, and the longer Lizzie was gone the more likely it was for someone to speak about matters no one wanted to mention. Matters that might not be relevant but still had to be checked.

God! He put his cocoa on the end table and rubbed his eyes. Someone had to talk. Someone always did. The criminal himself often told someone.

But what if the kidnapper—or killer—didn't talk to anyone around here? Spreading the search over four states made it even less likely that they'd hear anything. Too many people, some of whom wouldn't have a reason to care or wouldn't tell for a variety of reasons, like not wanting to get involved with the law.

Staring into the bleak reality of this case was like going down a black hole into nothingness. Staring into that empty hole eventually dragged him into a restless sleep. The black hole followed him into his dreams.

NOT FOR THE first time, Gage Dalton was finding it impossible to sleep. This time he didn't lie to his wife, Emma, claiming it was his back.

"The missing baby," she supplied without even asking him what was wrong. "For heaven's sake, Gage, you can't keep this up. Find a way to sleep or you'll be dead tomorrow."

He shook his head. "You go to bed. I'll manage."

"Then I'll stay up with you. Unlike you, I can call in sick tomorrow. Nora Jackson can handle the library."

He looked at Emma, taking in her beautiful face and thinking about her loving nature that had dragged him out of the dark pit his life had become all those years ago. Since then, life had touched her only lightly, making her all the more beautiful in his eyes.

"Do you suppose Nate would be up at this hour?" he asked suddenly. Nate Tate, the sheriff who had preceded him. The "old sheriff" as everyone referred to him, as they referred to Gage as the "new sheriff" even after all this time. That didn't bother Gage. It was a mark of respect this county continued to show the old lawman.

Emma looked wry. "Need a brainstorm, huh?" She glanced at the clock. "It's late but I'm sure he won't mind being dragged out of bed. He's that kind of man and he still hates being sidelined."

"Tell me about it. Besides, he knows this county better than I ever will. I swear he could name every person off the top of his head."

"He probably could, but he was born here, unlike you. Call him. If it bothers him he won't hesitate to tell you to get lost. He's never been one to withhold his opinion."

Gage finally rustled up a half smile, then reached for the landline. Every wise person out here kept one. Cell communications could be disrupted by any number of things. Which was why all his deputies carried satellite radios. SAT-COMS. Everything seemed to have an acronym.

Nate was on Gage's speed dial and the man sounded only mildly sleepy when he answered the phone. "Tate." Just as he had for years while he was sheriff.

"Gage," he answered. "Spare me some time?"

"The Chamberlain case, I reckon. Get your butt over here. I'll put on the coffee."

Gage kissed Emma goodbye with the always repeated "I love you." Because they both realized there was always a chance that one of them might not come home. The passing of years only strengthened that awareness. It might be the last time the words were spoken. The final memory.

Then he went out the door, pulling on a light jacket. The spring leaves were beginning to pass the feathery stage and become fuller. Beautiful in the daylight, creepier at night as the wind rustled them.

He had no room in his head to really notice, though. His thoughts, his worries, pushed him to Nate's house through the dark night, his official vehicle the boss of the roads he drove over. No traffic to argue with him tonight, however.

He made it to Nate's house in ten minutes over town streets toward the subdivision on the outskirts. Built after the Second World War in response to a pressing housing need and the GI bill, most houses here were small though well-kept. Nate's house was the exception. With six daughters, he'd long ago expanded to create space for his girls and all their friends. Practically a mansion compared to his neighbors' homes.

The porch light was on, as were lights inside the front of the house. As Gage pulled into the driveway behind the two family cars, Nate opened the front door, ready for him.

Age had added some lines to Nate's face and his dark hair had changed to silver but overall he looked like a man in great condition. He greeted Gage with a shake of hands. "Head for the family room. Still take your coffee black?"

"My stomach wishes I wouldn't, but yeah. Thanks."

The huge family room hadn't changed much over the years, even with the girls moved out. It had lost the bean bag chairs, however, replaced by some recliners that faced a large flat-screen TV. Gage sank carefully into one of the recliners and nearly sighed with relief. It eased his damaged body.

Nate returned with two large mugs of coffee. "Never thought I'd watch so much TV," he remarked, then took the other recliner. "Lousy case," Nate added. "I'm glad I'm not working it. How's Guy Redwing doing?"

Which meant that Nate still had his feelers out, was in touch with everything including who was leading the investigation. That gave Gage a probably exaggerated sense of support. He had sometimes thought this man would know if anyone sneezed in Conard County.

"Guy's doing great from everything I can tell."

Nate nodded. "I thought he would. Fine officer. I hope things are better for him. I remember when I hired Micah Parish, an old buddy of mine from Special Forces. Man did he get a load of BS around here. Well, until the day he took out a sniper in the bell tower of Good Shepherd Church."

"That would make a difference, all right. I'm not sure about how it's going for Guy along those lines. He doesn't talk about it at all. I suspect he's getting some bull, though."

Nate nodded. "Speaking of Good Shepherd, I just

got a ping tonight. Pastor Molly is returning early from her trip, should be here tomorrow."

"That's good. We could use her pastoral comfort right about now." Pastor Molly Canton was now married to the other detective in the sheriff's office, Callum McCloud. Callum had some business in his old hometown and Molly had taken some well-earned vacation time to accompany him. "Callum, too?"

"Just Molly. Woman's got a backbone of steel along with that gentle nature. Anyway, I'm sure you didn't come to discuss Molly."

Gage shook his head. "Heard any other whispers?"

"I wish. Never heard the grapevine so quiet in my life. Reckon Emma's told you the same."

"She has. It's strange."

"I'll grant you that. Never saw tongues quit wagging. Which I guess means that everyone is so shocked by all this, so disturbed, that nobody wants to be responsible for any rumor that could turn ugly."

Gage nodded. He sipped coffee and watched Nate do the same. Then he sighed. "Nobody's talking about anything, even in our interviews. You know as well as I do that the Chamberlains can't be perfect. No one is."

"Damn county's going to hell in a handbasket," Nate remarked. "Been saying that for years. When I grew up here, we didn't have the kind of crime we've been seeing the past years. Now a baby might be kidnapped or dead?"

Nate drained his mug then leaned back. "So tell me. What's going on and what do you want from me?"

"Ideas," Gage said bluntly. "Are we missing something? Are we going about anything in the wrong way?"

"You did the search, right? You're questioning people about anything they might have seen or heard about the Chamberlains. Tried to find if they have any enemies."

"And we've called for cadaver dogs."

Nate looked away. It almost seemed he winced. "Not good."

"No choice. Valerie suggested it." He paused. "You know who Valerie Brighton is?"

"Hell yeah. Now, *that* got the tongues wagging, including in the department. Some folks claim it shows that Guy ain't good enough."

Gage shook his head. "Bigots will find any excuse. Thing is, given she's a detective with a personal stake in all this, there's no way I could keep her out. Better to team her with Guy than have her trying to investigate on her own."

"Couldn't agree more. And folks'll simmer down once this case gets solved. I researched Valerie."

A crooked smile escaped Gage. "Why am I not surprised?"

"Well, I figure I got more time to look into her than you got." It was Nate's turn to smile. "So I did. Using access I'm not s'posed to still have."

Gage chuckled. "I didn't hear that."

"Figured you'd go deaf. Now Valerie. She's got a

brilliant record. Highest solve rate in robbery-homicide. A record most would envy."

Gage nodded. "That's good to know."

"Might could be this is a little different. She's *involved*."

"Thought about that. But *she's* the one who wanted the cadaver dogs. Cop thinking."

"True." Nate rose. "More coffee?"

"Natch."

Nate returned a minute later with freshened mugs. "Been thinking about this whole mess."

"I thought you would be."

"Any ideas I might not have heard?"

"Valerie asked Chet to look over his records for anyone who might have reason to hold a grudge against him. HIPAA is a problem. You wouldn't know if I can get a warrant?"

"Never had cause to get one, but law enforcement is probably allowed. Same as they can read your on-line chatting or phone info with a warrant. No damn privacy anymore."

Gage cocked his one functioning eyebrow. "You think that's bad?"

"Not for law enforcement. That's all I'll say, except you couldn't pay me to use any of them online social groups."

"Off the grid, are you?"

Nate snorted. "Like I said. So you think Chet might find something?"

"I'm hoping. You probably heard we're looking at kidnapping, too."

"No shock there."

"No ransom note, though. Strange."

"Somebody could have a different reason for taking the kid."

"That idea sickens me."

"Yeah." Nate fell silent. "Hell and damnation."

"We need just one thread to pull and we're not finding it."

"I'll think on it, Gage. Right now I ain't seeing a thing you ain't done. But if I come up with something, I'll let you know. And you keep me in the loop, too."

Gage had to be satisfied with that, but he was more satisfied they now had an additional brain, a good one, thinking about all this.

Another strand of hope, albeit slender. But just hope, not a lead.

He swore as he drove home and banged his palm on the steering wheel. He'd lost his kids to a car bomb intended for him. He'd nearly lost his mind. He knew how that felt to a parent.

And now he was losing his cool on this one.

HE WASN'T THE only one losing his cool. Not that Valerie had been totally cool since Lizzie disappeared, but it was getting harder to squelch her own grief even though it might hinder her in the investigation.

After she finally got an exhausted May into bed, she couldn't sleep herself. She paced the dimly lit house, her mind racing. Poking at everything they'd learned, trying to shake out more info. Seeking any hole they hadn't peered into.

She stared out the front window into the darkness and felt despair washing over her.

"God," she murmured. "Just a clue. Please, just one little clue to help us."

Chapter Eleven

The cadaver dogs arrived in the early morning. They were trained by separate owners but evidently willing to work together. Their owners looked a bit fatigued, having driven most of the night.

At nearly the same time, Kell McLaren arrived with his own K-9, both of them retired from the Army.

"Bradley," Kell said, "isn't a trained cadaver dog but he's damn good at chasing a scent. Any scent. Let him smell the baby's dirty clothes or a blanket. And let him sniff around for any other scent in that room. Won't take him any time to sort out a useful odor."

Guy didn't think that Bradley could do much more than the department's own K-9s, but he had to admit Kell's dog had a lot more experience. There wasn't much call for K-9s around here, except for searching for some idiot hiker who'd lost his way or managed to get himself injured. Or the occasional fool who tried to fly his small plane over the mountains.

"Go for it, Kell."

He took Kell and his dog into Lizzie's bedroom. May at once grew worried. "Another dog? He isn't…"

She clearly couldn't bring herself to speak the words.

"Nah," said Guy easily. "This one's Army trained. Probably better than ours." Maybe.

May looked relieved. "But the other dogs?"

"Same thing, but with more experience than ours."

May accepted it and returned to her living room, where she sat beside Valerie, who appeared washed out. Guy didn't expect much from her today.

"I've sent Connie Parish over to the hospital to do some interviews." He was past caring if May heard it. Besides, he reasoned, it wouldn't make Lizzie's disappearance any harder to take. Might even ease her mind to know something of what was being done.

Valerie nodded. A moment later, May nodded as well. The two were images of worn-out anguish.

"It's been too long," May said woodenly. "She can't be alive out there."

Guy sat facing the two women, controlling his expression. "Maybe we can find the exact place she disappeared."

May shook her head. "What good will that do?"

"We're trying everything, May."

"Yes," said Valerie. "We are."

May looked at her sister. "I know," she said finally. "I'm glad you're helping, Val."

Ouch, thought Guy, even though it wasn't fair. Why wouldn't May trust Valerie more than anyone else? Valerie had a bigger stake than the rest of them.

Besides, he was just a redskin cop. And how many times had he heard that in these parts? Or everywhere else.

Also not fair to May. He reined in his ugly thoughts that wouldn't help anyone, least of all himself. Instead he focused on the crushing burden May was placing on Valerie's shoulders.

He waited a few minutes, then when no more questions arose, he stood and looked at Valerie. "Get yourself some rest, Detective. You won't be much help right now."

She didn't argue, merely nodded.

That troubled him, too. He'd seen her fire, her determination. Was she giving up?

Kell McLaren's dog stood outside Lizzie's room, off lead now.

Kell said, "I don't know how much he found in addition to the baby's scent, but Bradley seems raring to go."

"Then let him." Although how Kell read that much in the dog, Guy had no idea. He had to trust Kell's experience.

The two went out the door. Unlike the cadaver dogs, also off lead, who were searching a wider area, Bradley kept lifting his head, sniffing, then sniffing the ground. He was searching for something different from the other dogs and he appeared to be seeking a scent apart from the others. He certainly didn't head toward *them*.

Maybe they'd get something out of this. He just hoped it wasn't the cadaver dogs who found it.

THE SEARCH CONTINUED throughout most of the day while Guy kept badgering the office about whether they'd gotten any kind of response to the widened Amber Alert. He knew they'd call him if they got even the slimmest lead, but he kept calling in anyway.

Connie returned from her expedition and motioned to him. He moved away from the house, hands tightening against disappointment. Not even the barest spark of hope ignited in him now.

Simple fact was he had begun to think about trying to find a psychic, because they sure as hell weren't getting anywhere this way.

"Well?" he demanded of Connie.

"Maybe something. Some of the PAs at the hospital know several people who got angry with Chet over the last few years. They won't say who, of course."

"Of course. Gage said he's looking into a warrant to break the HIPAA barrier. Don't know how long that will take."

"Judge Carter doesn't waste time when it's important."

"Never known him to. But there might be some difficulties here. Look, I'll stay here in case any of the dogs alert. You go over to see Gage and tell him what you learned. Maybe that'll be the probable cause the judge needs for a warrant."

"It can only help. Anyway, I haven't interviewed everyone. Gotta go back after shift change."

Guy watched Connie stride away then resumed

waiting. There was too much waiting in this case. He wanted some action.

He wanted a child back in her mother's arms and his hands around someone's throat.

A good solid punch would help, too, help exhaust some of the fury he dealt with. Except that it would be stupid beyond belief to hammer a tree and break his hand. Never had he wished more for a punching bag. But he couldn't afford the time to hunt one up.

He was involved in an endless hunt that required every ounce of patience he had, but he didn't have enough time.

Neither did that little girl.

In the late afternoon, he went into the house. Both women looked as if exhaustion had dragged them into sleep for a little while. Valerie's color had improved.

And sitting with them was Pastor Molly Canton, wearing her clerical garb of black shirt with white dog collar and black slacks. Molly was something of a bone of contention around this county, being a woman, but acceptance of her had grown after a few years. It was obvious she wasn't going away, no matter how much resistance she met.

Sort of like him, Guy thought.

"Listen," he said, "I'm gonna send Artie Jackson to Maude's. You folks want something to eat that doesn't come in a bakery box or a casserole dish?"

Molly smiled. Valerie managed a small one. May's face remained flat.

"We all need to eat," Molly said kindly. "Especially you, May. You have to keep up your strength for Lizzie."

At last May nodded.

With a little coaxing, Guy put together an order then went to hunt up Artemis Jackson, who was reaching break time from her shift in the trailer. She hated her first name, preferring to go by Artie. An athletic young woman, she wore her uniform well.

"Okay, Artie, here's the list for Maude. Throw in a meal for yourself. Chilly as it is, you need extra calories to stand out here."

Artie smiled, as much as anyone could in these circumstances. "Thanks."

"No thanks necessary. Trust me, the department is paying."

With a small laugh, Artie headed for her vehicle. Moments later she drove away.

Which left Guy pretty much alone, except for the deputy in the command trailer who was monitoring the location of the dog handlers.

Thinking about those cadaver dogs, Guy realized he'd never hoped so hard in his life that nothing would turn up.

AFTER DINNER, WHICH even May had eaten most of, Guy left the three women and stepped outside, mentally beating his head for ideas, solutions, anything at all in this intractable case.

He wasn't surprised when Valerie joined him a few minutes later.

"I'll go over to the hospital," she said. "Do some more questioning."

"You'll do no such thing," Guy answered.

She turned on him, blue eyes sparking. "How dare you?"

"Look, the people over there know who you are now, at least some of them. We're running up against a problem here, Valerie. I bet a lot of them don't want to talk because of your relationship to Chet and May. How could they say anything critical in front of you that might get back to the Chamberlains?"

She compressed her lips and turned her head away. She couldn't argue with that, thank God.

Damn, this woman was wrestling him into knots. And they weren't all about Lizzie. Her feelings were beginning to become his own. He felt her frustration, for sure. She needed to be doing something and right now couldn't. Well, neither could he.

After a bit, he said, "I told you I was sending Connie Parish over there. Everyone around here knows her. Spent her whole life here. What's more, they trust her discretion. Much as you don't want to admit it, Valerie, you've been away for quite a few years. They don't really know you anymore."

"Val," she said quietly.

"What?"

"Just call me Val. Everyone who knows me does."

So he knew her now? Maybe that was a compliment? Hell if he knew. He still wasn't sure he could trust her. His own form of bigotry, he supposed, a one-eighty from what he'd faced his entire life. Right now, though, he needed to get her mind on something else.

"So what's happening with that pup you rescued?"

She turned her head back to him. "I haven't checked."

"Then check. Seems to me you're in the process of adopting it."

Her lips curved upward ever so slightly. "I wish. My hours wouldn't be fair to a dog, though."

Well, he could understand that. "So think about a cat. It could probably endure your hours. Anyway, check on that dog. Might make you feel a bit better."

She nodded and pulled her cell phone out of her pocket.

Relief eased him, but only briefly. What could he come up with for another distraction? But distractions were far from his own thoughts.

Except her mouth. Man, that tiny smile. He closed his eyes. What was it they said about men thinking about sex six times an hour or more? But not right now. Absolutely not right now. Right now it felt loathsome.

"He's doing okay," she said when she disconnected. "Out of surgery and recovering. They're going to try to find someone to adopt him."

Sad, that. "It's amazing you rescued it. Considering you probably drove hell-for-leather to get here."

Her eyes widened. "How could I leave it, Guy? How could any feeling person?"

"Well, someone sure as hell did. Guess it was one of those people who don't have feelings at all for anything but themselves. Most folks around here know the value of animals. Most people depend on them one way or another."

"But not everyone. This is no utopia."

"True." Sad to say, but humans didn't seem capable of creating one.

He rocked on his heels, trying to think of something else. "You ever hear about the big program to colonize other planets?" He now had at least some of her interest.

"No, not really. Something about visiting Mars?"

He snorted. "Yeah, with plans to terraform it. Make it into another planet like our own. But that's not what I'm talking about. I'm talking about the bigger plan. The one that says we'll eventually have to escape Earth to save the human species."

"Wow," she said quietly. A spark of interest showed in her eyes.

"Yeah, I read an article about it recently. And all I could think was, what makes us think we're worth saving? Then they talked about how one of the biggest problems would be getting the thousands of people on a huge spaceship not to develop all kinds of problems with each other. You know, feuds, fights, all that."

"Wars," she said quietly.

"Exactly, because we all get along so well right now."

She nodded, that small smile appearing again.

"Anyway, I was getting more disgusted by the

piece, then this one scientist asked the question I was waiting for. He asked what makes us think we're so special that we need to be saved from extinction. He said there are eighty-eight million species on this planet. They don't deserve to survive?"

"Good point."

"So he concluded by saying we ought to just cram a small spaceship full of the most viable bacteria, send 'em out and let 'em evolve. Just the way they did here. In a few billion years they might evolve into us. Or into another species." He shrugged.

"That's a thought." Val's smile widened a shade.

"Sure is. On the other hand, how can we be sure we or the bacteria will arrive on completely dead planet? How can we be sure we won't become an invasive species that destroys all the life already there? Look what happened in the Americas when Europeans arrived."

Now her smile became broad. "I like the way you think."

He shrugged again. "Or maybe I see the whole world upside down."

"Maybe you have a right to, given your experience."

That observation took him by surprise. "Well, we haven't done such a great job taking care of *this* planet. Land us somewhere else and we'll do the same thing all over again. We don't seem to learn from our mistakes."

He let it go, aware that he was ranting, however quietly, a rant that came from his own culture.

Should he even try to explain that to her? Nah. She wouldn't understand. She'd probably think those beliefs were weird, or worse.

After a bit, Val spoke again. "Just more human superiority. When we're only a gene or two removed from chimpanzees. Have you ever seen them in a zoo?"

Guy shook his head.

"I did. Calm females looking rather disdainfully at a couple of male chimps that were acting pretty much like wild teenagers trying to impress the girls. I couldn't help seeing similarities."

Now it was his turn to smile. "Given what you see on the job, I'm not surprised."

She looked down, then glanced at the watch she wore. "I'm going in to get a drink since you've got me off duty. Want some coffee or tea while we wait here for what feels like forever? I'll bring it out."

"Thanks. Coffee if you don't mind."

Which left his own thoughts spiraling into the very real problem that wasn't going away, distractions notwithstanding. He called the office yet again. "Anything from the wider world?"

Velma's scratchy voice answered him. "We're doing what you said, calling every department we can find. Surprising how many there are in a state with so few people. Anyhow, nothing yet. All the federal and state forest rangers are on the lookout, too. Woods and brushland being searched everywhere. And we're just getting ready to start calling surrounding states."

"Tell 'em I don't care if it's just a wisp of something unusual. *Anything.*"

"I think they know that, Guy. But if you want, we'll call all of them again."

"Call. I need *something.*"

"Like I said, we're just getting on to neighboring states, too."

"Maybe it's time to start calling airlines. Except they probably see so many infants boarding there's no reason any would have stood out." He swore. If you looked at the numbers it was amazing how many people just vanished, never to be seen again. One little kid could do that even more easily.

VALERIE CAME OUT of the house carrying a tall coffee for Guy and two fingers of bourbon for herself. She rarely drank because she could be called out on a case at any time. But Guy had made it clear that she wasn't working right now. The waiting made it even more difficult.

She held her glass up to Guy. "Does this bother you?"

"Why would it? Never wanted the stuff. It's not like I'm a recovering anything."

She tried to smile but fear was rising in her again, like a tidal force that couldn't be denied.

Just then Guy's radio crackled with his call sign. He answered immediately. "What's up? Tell me it's not the cadaver dogs."

Valerie heart hit top speed, leaving her nearly breathless. God, no!

Then came the answer. "Kell McLaren's K-9. He's found the point where Lizzie Chamberlain disappeared."

Chapter Twelve

They got to the spot in less than five minutes. There was Kell, Bradley sitting right at the edge of the road, not all that far from the Chamberlain place.

Valerie and Guy jumped from his vehicle and trotted over to man and dog.

"Here," Kell said. "Right where Bradley is sitting. The child's trail vanishes."

Valerie felt her knees grow weak. Guy instantly reached out a steadying hand.

Guy spoke. "How can you be sure it's Lizzie's scent he's been following? If she was being carried, how could she leave a scent trail?"

Kell simply looked at him. "A million ways. Ask Bradley how he does it, not me. I just know he can follow scents that are days old. Maybe fuzz from a blanket drifted to the ground. Maybe the guy had to set her down occasionally."

"Well, that settles it."

Valerie drew a shuddering breath. "Kidnapping. At least she's not dead. We've got to tell May."

Guy scanned the area. "Not all that far from the Chamberlain house. What, a mile?"

"A little more," Kell agreed. "Whoever it was followed a circuitous route, though. Like he was afraid of being seen even in the dead of night."

"Or maybe the kid was crying," Guy said.

Valerie had thought of the same thing. Because Lizzie always cried when she was away from her mom. But why hadn't May heard a thing?

The question that had plagued her nearly from the beginning haunted her now.

GUY AND VALERIE returned to the Chamberlain house, a house that felt as empty as a tomb except for May and Pastor Molly.

May looked up immediately, her hands twisting Lizzie's blanket. "Anything?"

Valerie answered. "Kell McLaren's K-9 found where Lizzie disappeared. It definitely appears she was kidnapped."

May sagged and murmured. "Thank God. Thank God. She's not dead."

Valerie and Guy exchanged looks. There was no proof of that. None.

Valerie slipped outside with Guy and they held another brief meeting beside Guy's Suburban.

"No crying?" Guy said.

"No." Valerie's fists clenched and her neck appeared to stiffen as she turned her head to look into the deepening night. "She might already have *been* dead."

Guy blew a long breath between his lips. "Don't even think that way."

"Then why didn't May hear her cry? Why, Guy?"

He gave a short shake of his head. "You giving up?"

Her eyes blazed. "No, damn it. But all possibilities…"

"Have to be considered," he interrupted. "But how about you let *me* worry about the worst ones. Let's just find that little girl."

Val bit her lip. "Okay. Okay."

"Meantime shut your cop self down for just a little while. Give yourself a break. Hell, I don't know how you're walking this tightrope without falling."

"Funny, I had that image myself a day or so ago. I'm doing it because I have to."

He nodded. "Life's that way sometimes." He waited, knowing he was the only person she could share her fears with, all the million images and ideas that must be roiling her.

When she didn't speak, he turned to get into his vehicle. Then her voice stopped him.

"Guy?"

He faced her.

"I don't want to sit in there with May and do nothing at all. It'll make her feel worse if I'm sitting on my hands. Can I come with you?"

A new tension coiled in him, but he answered simply. "Sure, Val. Climb in."

VALERIE FELT AS if she was abandoning her sister, but she had to get away, just for a while, the need all the stronger because the investigation was turning up nothing. Because Lizzie had vanished into thin air and they had no idea where to look.

Because sooner or later May would begin to wonder why her sister was doing nothing. Because there'd be anger and confrontation, neither of which would do either of them any good.

She felt awkward about asking Guy to take her with him, but he hadn't seemed reluctant. She knew she was infringing on a professional relationship but it seemed a minor concern considering the entire situation. There'd been times in the past when she'd needed to be a cop with another cop. One who understood the worst sides of human nature.

Once she stood in Guy's small apartment, she wondered if she'd made a mistake. She hadn't thought about how this might affect him, the kinds of gossip that might make the rounds.

"You want me to go?" she asked him. "People might talk."

"People talk anyway, sometimes about things they know nothing about. I can offer you coffee, instant cocoa, or orange juice."

"Cocoa, if you don't mind. Maybe the milk will help me wind down."

"Sure." He stripped off his gun belt and headed for his bedroom. When he returned he'd shed his uniform for a chambray shirt and jeans. "Take a seat." He pointed to the recliner.

"But you…"

"Trust me, I can sit. So just relax as much as you can while I make cocoa."

It was a comfortable recliner, inviting her to put her feet up. She resisted. Leaning back and closing her eyes didn't strike her as relaxing at all.

Ten minutes later he returned with a cappuccino cup full of aromatic cocoa. "I added some cream." He set it on the end table beside her. "And so much for instant. Takes a whole bunch of time to dissolve that powder."

He turned and dragged one of his two kitchen chairs over, then got his own cup of chocolate, putting it beside hers on the single end table. He straddled the chair.

"You're gonna reach a breaking point, Val. I don't know how you can handle all this. Your personal concern, your need to be a cop in the midst of it. It's going to crush you."

She sighed and reached for the cocoa, sipping carefully. It was hot. "I've gotten near there a couple of times. I don't like feeling weak."

"Weak is the last thing I'd call you. And unfortunately I think you're right about your sister. At some point the blaming starts."

"Yeah. And that can leave permanent scars. I don't want that between us, although it probably can't be avoided if we don't find Lizzie soon."

She sipped more cocoa while staring into her personal hell. Lizzie. May. The fruitlessness of their hunt.

Guy spoke. "Connie said earlier that a few PAs

remembered patients getting really angry at Chet. She's gone back to the hospital to interview people after shift change. Haven't heard any more yet, but at least we've got one good reason to get that warrant."

"Thank God. I'd hate to think that a clue could be buried in patient confidentiality."

"I think Judge Carter will agree. He's always struck me as sensible."

"I seem to remember he's a good judge."

Clutching at straws, Valerie thought. All they had to cling to right now. Frustrating. Maddening.

"Gage went over to talk with the old sheriff. You remember Nate Tate?"

One corner of her mouth lifted. "How could I not? The man's a legend."

"Seems like. Anyway, Nate says you have an enviable rate of case resolution."

She shrugged a shoulder. "I'm not counting."

"You should. You should *trust* yourself, hard as it is right now. Your instincts are good. You're facing things you can barely stand to think about."

She shook her head. "The cadaver dogs?"

"Widening the search area tomorrow, but given what Kell found, those dogs are going to come up empty."

"God willing."

But another dead end. Someone had apparently taken Lizzie away in a car. She hated to think how many hundreds of miles the kidnapper might have traveled by now. "I'd give just about anything for a ransom note."

Guy's answer came slowly. "I'm not sure I would."

"Why?"

"Because any kind of ransom note implies violence."

"Against Lizzie," Valerie answered reluctantly. "No matter whether they get the ransom or not."

EVENTUALLY VALERIE DOZED off in the recliner. Guy waited a while, saw that at first she was restless but then calmer, more settled. More deeply asleep.

He chanced taking a shower, but when he looked in she was still asleep so he went to lie down on his bed. Meditation seemed to be his only possible escape into sleep but it didn't come easily.

Morning was creeping closer and he saw no help on the horizon. The sun would rise and nothing would change. Not unless some alert person or cop reported something unusual from somewhere.

But he couldn't afford to think that way. While the situation grew worse with every passing hour, he needed the hope that would keep him moving forward.

Maybe they'd get some useful info out of the hospital. He was counting on it.

But the first clue came with a knock on his door at nearly 4:00 a.m. Not his radio, but a knock.

Still half-dressed, he jumped out of bed to answer it. He saw Val starting to sit up, her eyes bleary.

Then he opened his door and saw the tall older man standing there. "Gray Cloud!"

The two men hugged with the affection of many years.

Gray Cloud entered, his presence seeming to dominate the entire room. No silver touched his long black hair, but the lines of wind and weather had marked him with their wisdom. His jeans were worn nearly white in places, his red jacket looking newer.

Guy made introductions. "Gray Cloud, this is Valerie Brighton."

Gray Cloud nodded. "The detective from Colorado. Sister to May Chamberlain, right?"

"Yes," she answered, rubbing sleep from her eyes. "Sorry if I'm intruding."

Gray Cloud shook his head and sat in the chair that Guy had earlier vacated. Guy pulled up his other one.

Then he explained to Valerie, "Gray Cloud is one of our elders, like a father to me. He's the guardian of Thunder Mountain."

A million questions filled Val's face but she didn't ask them. Good, this wasn't the time. A visit by Gray Cloud to town was rare. He certainly hadn't made his way here to speak about tribal or religious matters.

"Coffee?" Guy offered.

Gray Cloud shook his head. "I came to tell you one thing. A man with a small child was seen by one of our people. Out at the farthest reaches of our reservation. We sent a party to keep an eye on him but he was gone and hasn't come back." He looked at Guy. "I can take you there but it'll be on horseback."

"No problem, as you know."

Gray Cloud looked at Valerie. "You ride?" It was clearly an invitation.

"Yes."

"Then meet me at the old sawmill at dawn. I'll have horses and we'll set out. Maybe you can find a clue out there."

Then he rose and left with a farewell.

Valerie sat there, clearly wide awake now. "A clue? We have a chance at a clue?" She jumped up. "And who was *he*?"

"I told you, an elder. A nearly legendary one." He stood, too. "Let's get you back to the house. You'll want to get cleaned up and put on some clothes that will be better for riding, and warm enough in case we have to go up into the mountains."

AN HOUR LATER they were driving away from the early glow of the soon-to-rise sun and getting close to the old sawmill that hadn't functioned in over seventy years.

"What did you mean about that guardian thing?" Valerie asked.

"Guardian of Thunder Mountain," Guy answered, aware that he might make her see him in a different light than as simply another cop. An Indigenous one maybe, but still a cop. He hoped that didn't shift.

"Why does the mountain need a guardian?"

Well, he wasn't going to lie. "You must know something about Thunder Mountain."

"A little," she confessed. "There's an old gold-mining town up there, abandoned long ago."

"And the thunder?" he asked.

She hesitated. "A few times when I was in high school we went up to the mining town, even though we weren't supposed to. I...heard thunder a couple of times. Really loud thunder."

"Exactly." Guy hoped she'd leave it there. But of course she didn't. Every little detail mattered to a cop. To a good cop, anyway.

"What's this all mean, Guy?"

Here we go. He wasn't about to lie. "The mountain speaks to us through that thunder. After the Whites came to mine the gold, our forefathers decided the mountain needed protecting. Gray Cloud is the current guardian. Has been most of his life."

"I won't even ask how he protects it. I'd probably never understand. So it's holy ground?"

Guy nearly winced at the familiar White perception. "*Everything* on this planet is sacred to our way of thinking. Every rock. Every tree. Every animal or plant. It's all sentient. Thunder Mountain stands out the way some places do, but this mountain *speaks*. Let's leave it at that, okay?"

"I'd never understand anyway," she said quietly. "And I'm not being critical, just curious."

He could live with that, he supposed. It wouldn't surprise him, though, if she dismissed it all as superstition. Just about as superstitious as their churches.

Hell, it did no good to think this way. So what if this woman was peeling him open like the layers of an onion? Someone would have gotten around to it sooner or later, and he didn't mind that it was Valerie. Val.

When the sawmill came into sight, he forgot everything else. Gray Cloud stood there as promised with three pinto horses.

Gray Cloud spoke as soon as they got out of the Suburban. "We'll meet up with Jimmy Two Hands along the way. He's the man who saw the stranger with the small child."

They rode away from the sawmill as the sun began to brighten the day, although they still rode through deep shadows beneath trees.

VALERIE ENJOYED THE ride despite everything. The sway of the horse beneath her, the woods so redolent of evergreens with an earthy smell rising from the duff beneath their horses' hooves. Their saddlebags were full and she wondered what was in them but didn't ask. Gray Cloud carried a rifle in his saddle scabbard, Guy his pistol on his belt. Protection. Against bears or mountain lions maybe?

She found a measure of peace in those hours, admiring the beauty of nature, the beauty of the pintos, which were clearly well-kept. A rare space in time when she could draw a deep breath without aching. The tightness in her chest eased as it hadn't since before she heard the news about Lizzie.

They followed no road, but instead seemed to be riding along game trails. Gray Cloud certainly knew his way through these deep woods. Valerie had no doubt that she could get herself lost in ten minutes out here.

She also knew that the only thing that restrained her impatience was the hope that they'd find something useful at the end of this ride.

Guy drew up beside her a few times to ask how she was. He looked iconic, she thought, astride the horse as if he'd been born in that saddle. His long hair was caught at the nape of his neck in the way she'd become familiar with even though she wasn't used to seeing it on a cop.

"I'm fine," she always answered even though she knew that she was apt to become saddle-sore if this ride went on too long. She didn't care.

What wasn't fine was that she couldn't entirely let go of worry. The man and the child were gone now, Gray Cloud had said. They might find nothing useful at all.

Why the hell would the kidnapper have come to these mountains and woods anyway? Because he felt they would conceal him better? But why did he want to hide so far out of the way with Lizzie?

Questions. Too many questions. Her sense of peace slipped away.

After about three hours, which grew increasingly chilly as they climbed the slope, they came upon a mounted man who was waiting for them on his own pinto.

"Jimmy Two Hands," Gray Cloud said, then introduced Valerie and Guy.

"I know Guy," Jimmy said and didn't sound totally approving. Then he turned his attention to Gray Cloud. "The man is gone. The child with him. They were staying in an abandoned cabin a mile from here. There's some sign."

Sign? Valerie's attention perked.

"Why kind of sign?" Guy asked.

"You'll see."

More riding as Valerie's impatience grew, as any peace she'd found deserted her. After this they'd have to ride back to Guy's vehicle. Too long, especially if they found anything.

"Any news from Connie Parish?" she asked as Guy drew up beside her again. His radio hadn't crackled once so she knew there was no news. She needed to ask anyway.

"Not yet. She's probably found only more of the same. Mentions but nothing specific. I hope Judge Carter issues that warrant today."

She hoped so, too. Then there'd be so many records to examine. More information, she hoped.

At long last they saw the cabin in the distance, a decrepit box of logs. A small clearing filled with brush surrounded it.

"Whoever lived out here?" Valerie wondered.

"Some old guy," Guy answered. "A hermit who lived off the land."

"An ascetic," Gray Cloud corrected. "Forsaking all civilization to pursue inner knowledge and peace."

That sounded like an interesting story, Valerie thought. She wanted to ask Gray Cloud if he spoke with the mountain, but didn't dare. It was none of her business. Besides, she already felt as if she'd been permitted to know secrets and didn't want to press.

Nothing like a nosy White woman, she thought wryly. Which was probably how they saw her. White. She got it. Guy had been teaching her.

When they reached the cabin, Jimmy Two Hands dismounted and the others followed suit. Apparently these horses didn't need to be hitched or hobbled to keep them from wandering off. Reins were draped over their necks and they were allowed to browse.

Guy pulled two collapsed leather buckets out of his saddlebags and filled them from liter water bottles. For the horses. Well, that probably explained the full leather panniers.

"Before we go in," Jimmy Two Hands said, "let's walk around out here. There's information."

He pointed. "Off-the-road vehicle. He must have come up through that break in the trees. See?" He pointed out faint tracks leading that way.

"That would be an expensive vehicle," Valerie remarked. A clue in itself, perhaps?

Guy shrugged. "He could have rented it. We'll have to check into it."

Gray Cloud spoke. "He's also not allowed to use it here. How long ago, Jimmy?"

"Two days. See how the green parts of the brush are already straightening out?"

A whole lot of info from something that was barely visible to Valerie's eyes. Once it was pointed out to her, faint as it was, she could see it. She'd never have noticed by herself. Her impression of Jimmy Two Hands skyrocketed.

Once the trail of the vehicle had been marked by everyone's gaze, they approached the cabin's single door. It didn't even have a window, although a window would have been madness, given the winter.

Jimmy spoke. "There's not much inside, but enough to make me wonder. We heard about the missing child."

He retrieved a tactical flashlight from his own saddlebag. Gray Cloud pointed to Valerie's horse and she opened one of her own saddlebags, finding three flashlights in there. She passed them out.

"Move carefully," Guy warned. "Disturb nothing."

Jimmy gave him a nod of approval.

Inside, they found a wooden bench and a rustic lumber table with enough dust to suggest that it had been unused for years. A few empty cans and food packets. Then Valerie drew a sharp breath.

The dust had been disturbed on the bench and the table. Then Guy pointed. "The dirt floor has been messed with in that corner."

"SOMEONE STOPPED HERE," Gray Cloud reminded them. "It might mean nothing."

It might or might not. Narrowing the beam on her flashlight, she began a minute inspection of every part of the cabin, as did Guy. As if they were a forensics team.

Guy hoped for any clue beyond that someone had

been here. He was particularly interested in the area of the dirt floor that was a mess of boot prints, and the rough logs around it. He wanted any sign that a child had been here even though a witness had reported it.

He wasn't finding any though and cussed silently. A clue, damn it. A clue. He didn't know how much information it would give them except that Lizzie might have been here. If she had been, that wouldn't tell them where she might have gone, any more than Kell's dog's discovery had. But maybe they'd have something more useful to consider.

Then Jimmy spoke again. "Do you smell it?"

Valerie straightened and sniffed. There it was. "Soiled disposable diapers." Faintly she detected the smell of feces, ammonia and baby powder.

"Buried," Guy said and eyed the disturbed dirt. "Here maybe." He turned to Gray Cloud. "Any kind of shovel?"

Gray Cloud nodded, then went outside to whistle. One of the pintos trotted over. A minute later he returned with a collapsing shovel.

"Here," said Guy, pointing. "He trampled it for a reason." Then he took the tool from Gray Cloud and began digging. He imagined Val's heart was in her throat, as was his. They might find something worse than diapers in here. If the odor *was* diapers.

Val and Gray Cloud kept their flashlights on the area while Jimmy moved around the cabin, continuing to search.

"Lizzie's too old for diapers," Val said, her voice trembling.

Guy answered. "And maybe the kidnapper didn't know any better way to deal with the problem. I doubt he was lugging a kiddie toilet."

Then thunder clapped above them. A clear day but thunder clapped.

"The Chamberlain girl was here," Gray Cloud said, sounding as if he made a statement of fact.

GOD, VALERIE THOUGHT, was the mountain speaking to him? That thunder sure as hell shouldn't have happened. Her world began to spin as it tried to cope with a different reality but her gaze never left the hole Guy was digging.

Then it appeared: a dirty disposable diaper that was folded over. Soon Guy found more.

"The missing girl was here," Gray Cloud said again.

Valerie didn't doubt him for a moment although the diapers may have caused his statement. Her heart thundered as the mountain had. Now what?

She watched as Guy stopped digging and looked at Gray Cloud. "What else?"

God, Valerie thought again. Guy was asking for paranormal information from an elder. As if it were natural and right. Would he act on it?

Gray Cloud tilted his head. "Look east, Guy."

The return journey was faster. As if once having followed the path the horses felt comfortable in trotting back down it.

Her mind was totally blown but that hardly mattered. They'd found possible evidence that Lizzie was still alive. That was what truly mattered.

When she and Guy reached the Suburban, Gray Cloud led the pintos away. For their part, they sped in the vehicle down the nearly abandoned dirt road as fast as they dared.

Valerie, clinging to both hope and a fearful wonder, finally asked, "What happened in that cabin? God, the world just tilted. I can't..."

"Believe it?" Guy asked. "You don't need to. Soon enough you'll find a rational explanation or you'll forget about it. It doesn't fit in your world."

She bit her lip and fell silent. *Something* had happened. Eventually she returned to it. "The mountain spoke?"

"I heard it. Didn't you?"

"The thunder, yes. But how could it carry a message?"

"For those with ears to hear, it does. Does it really matter, Val? We found those diapers. Are you going to ignore what Gray Cloud said about Lizzie being to the east? Do you dare?"

No, she didn't dare ignore it. That much was true. There could be other explanations, for example that when they found the diapers it was easy enough for someone to say Lizzie had been there.

Guy was right. She was going to rationalize it away. She made herself stop. It wasn't respectful of her to dismiss his beliefs. Nor was it fair to Gray Cloud, who had taken the trouble to come to Guy about the stranger and child at the cabin. Whatever had happened, the part about Lizzie being to the east narrowed their search. Since they were finding nothing else, what harm could come from moving their search out to the east, away from the mountain slope?

But there had been that thunder, so sudden and out of nowhere. *That* was hard to explain.

Giving up, she returned to the most important matter: Lizzie.

GUY FELT VAL'S internal struggle as she sat beside him. He had no doubt where it was going to end and told himself it didn't matter.

There were two kinds of non-Native people. First, those who sought out Indigenous teachers to take them into a more mystical world. Sadly, most of those teachers were charlatans, claiming to be something they weren't, claiming an access to knowledge they didn't have. Not to mention that it insulted the beliefs of the Indigenous peoples. A week of sweat lodges and campfire stories in a haze of marijuana or the peyote that was legal only for Natives to use in religious practices. Plenty of money in it for these so-called teachers.

Then there was the other group of non-Natives, the researchers who studied lore and legend then dismissed it all as lore and legend without any basis behind it. Never giving any credence to the idea that those stories might not be apocryphal, but instead carried truth in stories that would easily pass down generation to generation.

He figured Val was going to settle firmly into the latter camp.

Oh well. She had *her* reality. He walked in it daily and understood it even though he didn't entirely lose himself in it.

Crossing a bridge of beliefs could never be without peril. All that mattered was that they heed Gray Cloud's statement that Lizzie was to the east.

That couldn't be ignored in *any* reality.

Chapter Thirteen

They arrived back in town by late afternoon and stopped first by the sheriff's office. Inside there was a buzz of activity, and without preamble Guy asked, "Anything?"

"Connie's zonked," Artie Jackson replied. "She *did* get enough information at the hospital to get the warrant in front of Judge Carter. We're hoping to have it issued in a couple of hours. You guys?"

Guy answered her. "Lizzie and her kidnapper seem to have been hiding in a cabin at the edge of the reservation. We found used diapers buried there. It was suggested that they're not far to the east of the cabin. I need to make up a new plan of action. Get operations ready to move in the morning. The cadaver dogs?"

"Nothing. Except some old bones that might have belonged to a long-ago miner or an Indian. No one knows how old, yet. Archaeologists are on their way."

"Okay then." He glanced at Valerie. "We can't start much until we have that warrant and we can't act on a new search plan until tomorrow. So I think Val and I are going to get some coffee and dinner from Maude's. I'll have my radio on in case anything turns up, but we both need a break."

"Long ride?" Artie asked.

"Long enough that I think Detective Brighton may well find it hard to move tomorrow."

Valerie was already stiffening up after the drive home, and her thigh muscles and seat were unhappy with her. As were a few other muscles. She sort of limped down the street to the diner.

She spoke just as they were about to enter Maude's. "Do you mind her using the word Indian?"

"Not as much as I mind redskin and Injun. It's okay, however untrue it is."

"Untrue?"

They found a booth near the back.

"Untrue," he repeated. "All because Columbus thought he'd found the West Indies. A slight correction was made with the name Amerindians, but not a good enough one."

"I can get that." Now it even hurt to sit, and she squirmed a little. He must have noticed.

"A hot bath," he suggested. "And some sports cream. We can hit the pharmacy for it after we eat."

"Longest time I've ever ridden a horse," she admitted. "I used to be a regular visitor to a stable where I could pay by the hour to ride. It was actually great, not just the riding but all they taught us about horse care, then made us do it ourselves. I loved it."

"But you don't do it anymore?"

She screwed up her mouth. "I became a detective. There's a huge downside to that promotion."

"On call 24/7," he agreed. "Kinda makes a hash of things."

"I wouldn't trade the job for the streets, though. Patrol cops spend more time being bored than I do."

He smiled faintly. "I spent a lot of hours driving around out there in a patrol vehicle. I sure got a good look at the countryside, though. Nights spent under the stars or sleeping in the back of my Suburban when I was too far out to return to the office."

"That sounds beautiful. I remember I could see more stars out there than any other place I've visited, except possibly Mesa Verde National Park."

He raised a brow. "I guess you didn't often sleep in the remote areas of the mountains."

She gave a small laugh. "You'd be right. It's a little unnerving when it's so dark you can't see the ground in front of your feet."

"Hence flashlights, lanterns, torches and campfires. Or moonlight."

"I love the moonlight."

"It'll sure wake you up if it hits your eyes while you're sleeping."

Val was trying, Guy saw. Trying very hard to tear her mind away from the pain and worry that tormented her. Well, he wasn't doing much better. He hated that they could do almost nothing right now.

"You know," he said as they finished eating, "it won't help to serve that warrant tonight. They'll be on night staff at the hospital, administration gone for the night. And what will we get anyway? A handful of names to eliminate because I'll bet my badge that the man we want won't be much easier to find than he is now, even with a name. He's gone."

She looked down at her nearly empty plate then pushed it aside. "Let's get some coffee to go. Then I need to get to my sister. God, I can't imagine what she's going through."

"I think you can," he said as he picked up the bill. "You're most of the way there yourself."

Guy dropped Valerie off at the Chamberlain house, ignoring a wish to take her back to her place. Just so he could keep an eye on her, he told himself. But he was getting past the point of believing that was all it was.

"I'll sketch out a search plan for tomorrow," he assured her.

He watched her limp up toward the front door. That woman was going to find it almost impossible to walk tomorrow.

Then he drove to the office to study maps. Online mapping wasn't going to work for this.

INSIDE, VALERIE FOUND that Pastor Molly was still there, dozing in a chair. Molly stirred the instant Valerie entered.

"May is in bed," Molly said. "She's so worn out it's a wonder she wakes up at all. Chet was here for a while, then got called in for a delivery. Complicated, he said."

Hardly surprising, Valerie thought. Chet was always being called in. At least he had something to focus on other than his worry and anguish. May had no such escape.

Valerie sat on the couch with the latte Guy had bought her. "I'm sorry. I didn't think of getting one for you."

Molly looked wry. "I know my way around a coffeepot. Even that fancy espresso maker your sister has. I'm fine and caffeinated to the gills."

"We didn't have any coffee on the ride today. I'm making up for it."

Molly tipped her head. "How'd the trip go?"

"It was long. We *did* find diapers buried in this old log cabin. Reasonably fresh. And tracks of an off-road vehicle that came in and left."

Molly nodded. "I guess that helps. You know when they were there?"

"Left a couple of days ago, Jimmy Two Hands said."

"That long ago? I mean, getting the word here…"

"It's a long way out," Valerie answered. "Took us three hours to get there on horseback. Given the location, I doubt it would have been any faster on an ATV."

Valerie sipped her latte, grateful for its warmth, its flavor. Caffeine started to wake her up. "God, I'm sore from that horse."

Molly laughed quietly. "I've heard about it, but never tried it."

Valerie drank more coffee, then chewed her lip,

hesitating. "Molly?" She had a question that wouldn't go away.

"Yes?"

"You're a religious person. I think…" Again Valerie hesitated. Molly waited patiently.

"I don't know if I'm supposed to talk about this," Valerie continued a minute later, her heart tapping nervously. "But while we were out there, we heard a loud thunderclap."

"That's strange. There isn't a storm in sight."

"Which made it astonishing. Then… Gray Cloud spoke. He said with certainty that Lizzie had been the child in the cabin, and that she was east of there."

Molly frowned faintly. "What are you trying to say, Val?"

"That Guy believes that the thunder speaks to Gray Cloud, who is, by the way, the guardian of Thunder Mountain."

"And that troubles you?"

"I don't know what to think. Guy said the thunder speaks to those who have ears to hear it. How do I process that? Is it even remotely possible?"

"You're asking either the right or the wrong person about that depending on your beliefs." Molly smiled. "I believe God speaks to us through our hearts and minds. Sometimes it pops into my head as clear as if I were being spoken to. Not often, but it's happened to me a few times. Not just a feeling, but clear *words*."

Valerie leaned forward, listening.

"You can believe me or not," Molly continued.

"Does it fit your own beliefs? It fits into mine. So about Gray Cloud? I'd say that thunder speaks to him. I'd say the breeze breathes secrets and the creaking of trees may be filled with meaning. I suppose that would shock my parishioners if I said it that way, but ears to hear? Yes."

Valerie blew a long breath and leaned back. "Thanks, Molly. I guess Gray Cloud might hear the thunder speak."

"It's all God's creation. Who are we to limit the Almighty?" Molly rose. "I'm going to make myself some coffee."

Halfway to the kitchen, she paused and looked back. "Val?"

"Mmm?" Valerie was still trying to absorb what Molly had said.

"I told you that sometimes I hear God as clear as the spoken word. Wasn't so long ago that I had one of those experiences."

Valerie raised her head. "Yeah?"

"Yeah. I was praying about whether I should take this job. Praying hard, I might add, feeling deeply pulled toward it but resisting the tug, not sure I was strong enough or worthy enough for this task. I kept begging for guidance. Then, as clear as anything, a voice in my head said *I'm telling you but you're not listening.* So here I am."

Wow, Valerie thought. Just *wow*.

Chapter Fourteen

Guy had spent hours poring over terrain maps, determining the possible paths the kidnapper's ATV could travel, figuring out where search parties should move and whether they should go on foot or by horse or their own ATVs.

He wasn't going to leave even a square yard unaccounted for, but plans still had to be made, as did a decision about whether to start with a wide cordon moving in toward the log cabin or whether they should spread out from it.

He snagged a couple of hours of sleep in one of the cots at the back of the building, then dove in again. The list of searchers he needed was massive.

He counted up horses and ATVs, as well as seasoned hikers who would be prepared for the sudden weather changes that could happen in and around the mountains. Prepared to take care of themselves if they became injured.

The numbers were staggering, especially considering that if the kidnapper had ditched the ATV and driven away in an auto, he could have traveled quite a distance. But he hadn't yet. What was holding him in the area?

If they could find an answer to that question this hunt might get a whole lot easier.

But they had more questions than answers and had since the outset. Even the Amber Alert was bringing in no hints.

Well, plenty of people were looking in more distant areas. He had to concentrate on his own patch.

Given the massive numbers of horses, vehicles and people he needed, he started a phone tree going at dawn, each person contacted asked to contact two more and so on. The surrounding ranches sure had plenty of horses and vehicles. The park and forest services might have lists of regular hikers.

He settled on a staging area and arranged as best he could for supplies anyone might need. He ordered the command trailer moved to it along with its generators.

He didn't know if this county had ever organized such a large operation, but the knowledge wouldn't help him now.

This was a whole new ballpark, and not even Gage, with all his experience, seemed to know if this had happened before. If it had, he had never heard of it, nor had the old sheriff, Nate Tate.

A first. He almost wished he wasn't spearheading it.

VALERIE AWOKE SO stiff that when she tried to sit up to get out of the bed, she groaned. Somebody lead her to the ibuprofen, please.

And here she'd thought she was in such great condition. Not.

She found ibuprofen in the medicine cabinet and popped three, regardless of the directions. She could barely wash herself in the hot shower, had trouble toweling herself dry. Pulled her clothes on with more stifled groans.

Sheesh. She left the bedroom hoping the ibuprofen would start working soon.

She found May sitting on the sofa once again. Molly was there, freshly dressed so she must have found time to slip away during the night. Today she wore an ankle-length skirt instead of slacks.

Coffee smelled fresh in the air, so with a mumbled "Good morning," Valerie headed straight for it. With her mug full, she limped back to the living room and joined the two women.

May looked at her hopefully. "Molly says you found something?"

Ack. No way to be sure except for Gray Cloud's declaration and she still didn't know if he was right. She looked at Molly, then felt her own certainty. She had to share it with May.

"We're pretty sure the kidnapper had Lizzie in a small log cabin on the slope of Thunder Mountain. Guy is working on a new search plan."

"Had?" May repeated. "He took her away again?"

"He's hiding," Valerie said gently. "He doesn't want to be found."

May closed her eyes. "I can't believe someone would do this for no reason. Why no ransom note?"

"It's not for money," Valerie said with conviction. "This guy's got another reason but we don't know what. What we *do* know for sure is that as of two days ago Lizzie was alive."

"How can you know that?" May demanded, her eyes moistening.

"Because we found diapers. Fresh ones."

"Diapers? Lizzie doesn't wear diapers! It can't be her!"

Valerie reached for her sister's hand and quoted Guy. "And this guy can't be carrying a kiddie toilet around with him. Can he?"

May drew a ragged breath. "I guess not. But Lizzie won't like it. She's so proud of having grown-up panties. Oh, God, she must be so scared! Hating it all. Wondering where I am and why I don't come for her!"

There was no way to dispute that. And no way to evade the likelihood that once they got Lizzie back she was going to be scarred. Maybe for life.

Valerie shoved that aside. Years of counseling might be ahead for Lizzie but all that mattered right now was getting her back healthy and safe. The *only* thing that mattered.

Molly spoke. "May, wherever Lizzie is right now, she knows you love her. She hasn't forgotten that."

"But she must be wondering." May dropped her head. "I can't take this anymore. Lizzie probably can't either."

Molly answered. "Children are a whole lot more adaptable than adults. More accepting of the way things are. You're probably having a far worse time than she is."

Valerie looked at Molly, thinking the pastor couldn't possibly know that, even if it sounded likely given that the kidnapper was taking care of Lizzie well enough to have provided and changed diapers.

But they were apparently the right words for May. She lifted her head. "I hope so. Oh, God, I hope so."

GUY ARRIVED A short time later, looking like a man who was pushing past the limits of fatigue. His voice, though, was as strong as ever.

"A new search party is gathering," he told them. "We're going to have a hundred people or more with horses and ATVs arriving soon, along with a bunch of experienced hikers. And Connie Parish is taking the warrant and a team to the hospital. Administration will begin searching records."

"Oh, thank God," May whispered.

Guy turned to Valerie. "Want to come to the staging area with me, or would you rather join the team at the hospital?"

Valerie didn't hesitate. "I'll go to the staging area."

OF COURSE SHE'D come to the staging area. There'd be more action out there and she couldn't bear the thought of shuffling through mounds of paper, looking for a needle in a haystack. Even though that was often a part of her job, it was a part she didn't want to do just then.

Lizzie was out there. If she took Gray Cloud at his word, as Guy apparently had, then east was the best place to look. Guy was right about the paper search, too. The kidnapper was hiding and a name wouldn't help them much. They still had to find him and Lizzie.

The ibuprofen had begun working and she carried a small bottle of it with her. In case she needed to move quickly, she couldn't afford to be hampered by aching muscles. Although if adrenaline kicked in for some reason, she'd move anyway. And fast.

The staging area took her breath away. It was already a jumble of horses and riders, ATVs and backpackers, all apparently waiting for directions. It wasn't long before Guy had the terrain maps laid out on a long folding table, and with men and women around, separated by means of transport, he began pointing out the directions he wanted them to take.

Valerie got the feeling that these searchers knew the area well enough to simply nod when Guy told them where he wanted them to head.

Valerie turned around slowly, surveying the land she could see. Here the rolling hills that filled most of the county had grown much steeper as they butted up against the mountain. Still full of woods. Ravines and gullies sliced through them. The seemingly gentle roll of the land was deceptive only because the slope of the mountain itself looked so much more treacherous.

As groups of searchers began to spread out, the police K-9s arrived along with Kell and his dog Bradley. Only a few dogs when all was said and done, probably because the sheriff couldn't afford to have very many. K-9s were expensive.

No, not very many K-9s, but each would be an important help. The dogs were assigned to mounted groups, which might easily miss something. Their handlers mounted and went with them.

But the ATVs went alone, something that worried Valerie. If they moved too fast, they could easily miss something. Then there were the hikers. How much terrain could they cover?

Still, the group was impressive in its size, and Valerie tamped down her worries. She was impressed that so many had turned out to help, taking themselves away from other duties and pursuits. All of them set out for rough terrain, places where a child or an ATV could be hidden.

Except that Lizzie was so tiny. And what if the kidnapper had abandoned his vehicle?

It didn't bear thinking about.

Coffee urns had been set up, plugged into the generators, and mounds of dried foods had diminished as the searchers stuffed them into their saddlebags, backpacks and ATV compartments. Then Valerie watched as they disappear over hills and into woods.

So many of them. She still felt a sense of disbelief. And she desperately wished she was physically capable of going with them.

Then Guy nudged her. "Look."

A new group of at least a dozen mounted men approached, among them Jimmy Two Hands and

Gray Cloud. Gray Cloud drew rein in front of Guy. "We're not the only ones among us who are searching. Where do you most need this group?"

Guy looked up at him. "Where are the others?"

"We've been combing the reservation since yesterday morning. Dozens of us. But this team? Where would we be most useful according to your plans?"

Gray Cloud needed only the quickest look at the map and where Guy pointed. With a nod he heeled his horse. With him, fifteen men rode away.

"I can't believe..." Valerie started to say, then sank onto a folding chair.

"What? That so many people give a damn about what happens to a small child they don't even know?"

She shook her head. She didn't know how to explain her incredulity. It was amazing. Overwhelming. Something she had never expected to see and would probably never see again.

Guy disappeared into the operations trailer while Val remained outside. It was a beautiful morning, crisp, clear, perfect. An army had just headed out in nearly every direction to seek Lizzie. An army of volunteers.

The only reason she was sitting here rather than going out with one of the groups was that she'd killed herself riding yesterday. She couldn't mount a horse yet. She doubted she'd do more on an ATV than hang on and groan. As for hiking...well, she was still limping.

Maybe she should have gone to the hospital after all. Reading through patient records would be more useful than where she was now. She hated the feeling of uselessness.

Guy eventually returned and sat in a folding chair beside her. "How are you holding up?"

"Angry that I got so saddle-sore yesterday that I'm no help today."

He shook his head a bit, adjusting his tan uniform Stetson on his head. "There are plenty of people out there. You wouldn't be able to add a thing. Anyway, the cordon is starting to narrow. Nothing yet."

Valerie wasn't surprised. She would have expected him to burst out of that trailer if there'd been any news to share with her.

"If they don't find her..." She let the words trail away. They were obvious.

"Connie says they've managed to get a few names out of staff members and their files are being examined."

Valerie sighed. "Like you said, how much good will that do?"

"Depends," was all he answered.

Eventually she said, "I'm sorry I doubted that Gray Cloud could understand the thunder."

He turned his head, looking at her. "What brought that on?"

"A story Pastor Molly shared with me. Maybe more importantly, something she said along with it."

His gaze grew more intense, those dark eyes pinning her. "Which was?"

"She believes the wind whispers and the trees

creak, and those with ears to hear understand. Like you said."

"Anything else?"

This seemed important to him and she understood why. She had doubted his cultural beliefs and now he wanted recognition from someone outside it. "She said it's all God's creation and asked who are we to limit the Almighty?"

Guy nodded and returned his attention to the forest that reached up above him. She noticed for the first time that the evergreens cradled hardwood trees that were just beginning to burst with spring life.

"Life," she said, her mind wandering as it noted the trees, "is both important and precious. *All* of it."

"But right now Lizzie is the most important of all."

Tears pricked her eyes but she didn't give in to them. "I can't thank you enough, Guy. I really can't."

"No need. Look at all the people who are trying to help. Every one of us wants to find that little girl."

"I see that." Her heart nearly burst in a way very different than from grief and fear and anguish. "I don't think I've ever been filled with so many conflicting emotions."

"You're on one hell of a roller coaster ride."

He offered a hand and Valerie took it, nearly clinging to the comfort of his touch, feeling less alone, less tossed on a stormy sea.

Guy glanced at her repeatedly from the corner of his eyes. She was nearing something, he thought. Nearing a breakdown? Or something else? All he knew was that he was worried about her. The rapids they rode in this river could crush her. No amount of experience and training could overcome how personal all of this was to her.

He squeezed her hand gently but didn't let go. If she needed a rock to cling to right now, he would be that rock for her. Whatever it took.

"Lizzie's safe," he said presently.

"I haven't heard the thunder."

He eyed her sharply. "I just know it, Val. I *feel* it. Whatever is going on, this man doesn't want to hurt her. Those diapers prove it, but you don't need me to tell you that."

"No," she agreed quietly. Once again Guy was right.

"So she's safe," he said. "Alive and well, although she's probably not happy right now. She's being sheltered by a sick mind but sheltered regardless."

The wind quickened suddenly and she looked up for the first time. "Oh, God."

Guy followed her gaze. "A storm. A freaking storm." Overhead, gray clouds roiled, coming nearer.

"That'll end the search."

"I doubt it. I seriously doubt it. Those folks out there are determined."

This time she could only hope he was right. "How are the searchers being tracked? Or are they?"

"In this part of the world, satellite phones are common. We're tracking them."

She nodded, hanging on to the reassurance. What else did she have?

Thunder rolled down the mountain and he heard her catch her breath. Rain couldn't be far behind and would chill the kidnapper and his precious burden if they had no shelter.

"God," Val said. "Can it get any worse?"

It could. Guy knew that and was sure she did as well.

He stared up into the boiling clouds and wondered if Gray Cloud heard anything this time. He hoped so.

A COUPLE MORE hours passed fruitlessly. Then Guy's radio crackled. It was Connie.

"We've got a dozen names, Guy," she said. "I'm sending people out to question them now."

"Read me the names," he said to her, and listened to the list.

Then she said, "Margolis. Phillip and Etta Margolis."

Guy rose instantly to his feet. "The Margolis place is closer to us than to you, Connie. I'm heading that way."

The rain began to fall, just gently. It was going to get worse.

As if summoned, Gray Cloud and his pinto emerged from the growing mist of rain. Guy waited impatiently for the elder to draw close.

Sitting straight in his saddle, Gray Cloud pointed. "That way. One of us found the ATV in a ditch hidden beneath tumbleweed. The girl is alive." He slid from his saddle and approached the maps that were still laid out on the table. He bent over them, studying them, then pointed to a spot with his index finger. "Here." Then he mounted again and headed in that direction, off the rez into a world more hostile to him.

Guy's heart sank. That wasn't in the direction of the Margolis place. Gray Cloud had indicated ranch land, wide-open spaces of brush and greening grasses.

For once he chose to ignore Gray Cloud. He poked his head into the ops van and said, "I'm going to be away from the staging area for a while. Radio me." Without another word, Valerie in tow, he headed for his Suburban.

They had to start somewhere and the mention of the Margolises might be the only concrete information they could get.

He knew exactly where the Margolis couple lived. In the past he'd been called out there several times for domestic disturbances. Phillip Margolis was a slimeball.

ETTA MARGOLIS SAT at her kitchen table, a cold cup of hot chocolate in front of her. She didn't want to walk to the mailbox, fearing another note from Phillip. Instead she used the growing storm as her excuse. When rain started to fall, her excuse became a good reason.

She had long since grown to distrust her ex-husband. Over the years she had learned that he was willing to lie and cheat, and that he could become violent, oftentimes with little reason that she could tell.

She was well rid of him. She never wanted to see or hear from him again.

But those notes niggled at her. What the hell was Phillip up to now? And how did it involve her?

That stuff about having found a kid for them increasingly bothered her. Surely he hadn't done something wrong. Not something like that. Beating her, throwing things, cussing, conning, stealing when he could, justifying every horrendous thing he did? Yeah, that was Phillip.

But she still believed there had to be some things he wasn't capable of.

They had already lost one baby. Etta didn't want another.

Chapter Fifteen

Guy and Valerie reached the end of the forest service dirt road and turned onto a county road that was in little better condition. County funds had managed to pave a lot of outlying roads, but maintaining them was expensive, too. Guy had to steer around a lot of potholes, the result of winter, slowing the trip more than he would have liked.

Valerie spoke as they jolted along. "What's with the Margolises? Why did you jump into high gear when you heard the name? It's not just that it's closer for you to reach, is it?"

He gave a slight shake of his head as they rose over another sharp bump. "I know that couple in all the wrong ways. Too many calls for domestics."

"Hell," Val said quietly. "So they're dangerous?"

"In this way? I don't know. I'm sure it's not Etta, but her husband, Phillip? I'm not as sure about him." He paused, steering them around a pothole. "That man is violent and it doesn't take much to set him off, near as I can tell. Full of rage."

Valerie didn't speak, but a glance at her told him she had paled.

"Listen," he said, "this is probably a wild-goose chase, but I *can* get there faster than anyone else. Keep in mind that whoever has Lizzie is taking care of her. Okay?"

"Okay."

"I just want to clear the plate of this one item. That's it."

"I understand. And then?"

"Then we'll see."

VALERIE STARED OUT the Suburban's window at the countryside that jolted by. They were leaving behind the location where the search was ongoing, and driving away from the area that Gray Cloud had indicated. Had the kidnapper really moved again? Now Gray Cloud and his team had found the ATV. Why was Guy ignoring that?

Was she clinging to the thinnest of straws, a man who heard thunder speak and said Lizzie was alive?

She turned her head to look at Guy. His strong face had settled into lines of stone. He was holding himself in tightly.

Guy was a cop, she thought. Following the most important hard evidence rather than his elder. She judged the tug between two worlds must be hard for him, but he still chose the path of a true investigator.

The gentle rain was falling here, too, enough of it to make Guy lean forward to see obstacles in the road. She heard another roll of thunder and wondered almost wildly if that would change the direction of the search again. She felt as if she were becoming untethered from reality and tried to convince herself it was just stress and lack of sleep.

Then she looked again at the man beside her and realized that Guy was firmly tethered to reality, even if they were two slightly different realities. She gazed at him, envying his strength. He straddled such a fine line while remaining steady. Steadfast.

She wondered what she would have done without him.

The wipers continued to *thwap* and the rain grew heavier. Lizzie was out there somewhere. In the cold and wet. She could only hope the SOB had her inside and protected.

When she saw a few flakes of snow begin to drift down, she nearly wanted to scream. Did it have to keep getting worse?

"Not much farther," Guy said almost abruptly.

He seemed to be getting angry.

"Do you think Lizzie will be there?"

"I don't know. I'd like to think Etta would have acted if Phillip had showed up with a kid. But I don't know for sure. He damn near killed her a couple of times."

Val knew such situations intimately. "She'd be terrified."

"She's *lived* terrified. Never could get her to press charges, though. I tried. Kerri Canady tried. It seemed all she wanted was to put an end to the abuse, temporarily anyway. But fear still held her prisoner."

Valerie had often thought the story of abuse to be a sad one. People wondered why the abused spouse didn't just leave. Those people didn't know how such terror could become an iron cage.

"There's the road. I guess you'd call it a driveway." He swung the vehicle sharply to the left and they began bouncing down an even worse road, at the end of which waited the Margolis house. About a mile away, Valerie judged. A lonely house in the middle of nowhere.

Her hands knotted into fists. *Please let Lizzie be there.*

GUY PULLED RIGHT up to a battered porch, tugged a rain cover over his cowboy hat and hurried to climb out. Valerie joined him, heedless of the growing downpour.

Guy pounded on the door. No gentle knock of announcement, but a full police banging that demanded attention.

Half a minute later the door opened, showing a thin, bedraggled woman who bent as if she were old.

"Deputy Redwing," she said dully. "I didn't call you."

"Let us in, Etta. We need to talk."

Etta nodded and stood back from the door, giving them entry. Inside, the small house spoke of deep poverty, everything worn out, the walls peeling, the wood floors warped.

"This is Detective Valerie Burton," Guy told Etta. Then he waved a hand. "Etta Margolis."

"I got coffee," Etta said nervously.

"No thanks," Guy answered. "Where's Phillip?"

"I don't know." Etta sagged into a chair at a battered kitchen table that was part of what might be called the living room. Behind her was a stove, a small slab of counter and a sink with a hand pump. "I don't know."

"Why don't you know?"

Etta shook her head. "Ain't seen that bastard in more'n two years."

Now Guy pulled out two chairs, taking one himself and waving Valerie to the other. "That's good, Etta."

"Damn straight," the woman said more firmly than Valerie would have expected, given that she looked as weak as a frail bird. "I swear if he shows his face around here ever again, I'll get the shotgun. I shoulda got it years ago."

"I wouldn't have blamed you," Guy answered. His voice had grown kind, as if he felt badly for this woman.

"The rest of the law would've." Etta regarded him. "Why you want Phillip?"

"Just need to ask him a few questions."

Etta shrugged. "Ain't got no idea what that man's up to now."

"I guess not." Guy paused. "You know we're looking for a little girl who disappeared a few days ago. Chet and May Chamberlain's daughter."

Val saw Etta pale even more, if that were possible. Her heart started galloping when the woman's eyes slid away. Etta knew something.

"Didn't hear. Their baby's gone?"

"Somebody took her."

It seemed a long time before Guy spoke again. "I heard you and Phillip got really angry when you lost your baby."

Etta sagged a bit. "*Phillip* got angry. He hit me a lot. Blamed me and the doctor for it."

Valerie leaned forward, needing to hear more. She spoke carefully. "But *you* didn't get angry?"

"I was too busy hurting. Grieving. That man wouldn't give me no space to cry, just blamed me until I couldn't find a tear left."

God, what an image, Valerie thought. What an awful, horrible image. How terrible this woman's life had been. "I'm so sorry," she said.

"It's done. Gone. That man took to his heels cuz I said I'd shoot him in his sleep if he didn't stop. Guess he believed me." Then Etta looked at Guy. "The baby was kidnapped?"

"That's how it looks. Thought I'd check with you in case Phillip…"

Etta interrupted him. "He might coulda."

Guy heard Valerie draw a sharp breath. Now she'd be hanging on tenterhooks, not that it would do any good. Sadly, he believed Etta when she said she didn't know where her husband was. No help in that.

But he pressed ahead with questioning her. "You have any reason to think that? Any idea at all?"

Etta gave a jerky nod. "Got two notes from him. First one just upset me, but I didn't make nothin' of it. Threw it in the compost without reading it. Then I got another one and thought he'd lost his mind. If he ever had one."

Guy heard Valerie breathing quickly now. They were on the edge of something. How much good it would do he couldn't yet know.

"The second note," he prompted gently.

Etta looked at him, and for the first time expression creased her face. Alarm? "Said he found a baby for us. Couldn't think how. Thought he was lyin' again. Nobody'd let that man adopt a kid. But..." The word trailed off.

Now Guy was leaning forward a bit, his deliberately relaxed posture gone. "Where'd the note come from? Do you still have it?"

"Out with the compost like the first one."

"Did you see a postmark?"

"Don't recall." Then Etta started shaking her head and her whole body began to rock. "Shoulda kept 'em. Now they's on the compost heap. Ain't nobody gonna find 'em now." Then tears started to roll down her face.

"Kidnapping a baby," she mumbled. "Sweet Mother Mary, that man's eviler than Satan hisself."

As soon as they were back in the vehicle, Guy reached for his SAT phone.

"I need two things yesterday," he told dispatch.

"I need an urgent bulletin put out on Phillip Margolis. He might have Lizzie Chamberlain. Then I need three or four people out here to go through a compost heap looking for envelopes he might have sent to his wife. I need a postmark."

An affirmative answer crackled back to him.

Then he added, "Oh, and a third thing. Tell ops to start reeling in the search parties. I have information that's going to redirect us. I'm headed that way now."

Val looked at him. "What Gray Cloud said? I thought you were ignoring him."

Guy shook his head. "Never wise to ignore that man. I prioritized. We got our information, such as it is, and the gear is ratcheting even higher."

He pounded his hand on the steering wheel.

"If we hadn't found those diapers yesterday, I'd be scared to death for Lizzie now. Phillip Margolis. A damn grenade just waiting for someone to pull the pin."

Then he jammed the Suburban into gear and they took off again, this time with less respect for the condition of the roads and the heavily falling rain.

Thunder boomed again, louder and more threatening. Overhead, the skies darkened and wept copious tears.

PHILIP MARGOLIS HUNKERED down in the remains of a sod hut built ages ago by some settler. It didn't have much inside it, but at least it still had a roof.

He'd never have guessed a kid could cry so much. The sound was driving him out of his gourd. Changing her diapers didn't help. Wrapping her in stolen blankets, including a ratty one he'd had for himself, didn't help. Mashed canned food didn't help.

If he hadn't promised the kid to Etta he'd have left it somewhere for the coyotes.

He could hardly believe now that he'd ever wanted a kid so much that he'd raged like an angry bull when they lost it. If a kid this old could make such a ruckus, he figured a brand-new one would be even noisier and unhappier. And every bit as stinky.

He'd have to get to a store soon. All the food he'd stuffed into his beat-up old truck was getting sparse. He needed more of those damn diapers, too. He wondered desperately if candy would make that kid shut up.

For the first time in his life, Phillip Margolis pondered whether he'd made a bad plan. All to get that damn woman back, a woman who made him mad but at least took care of him to his own specifications. The only good thing he could say about Etta. How had he figured she'd come back to him just for a shrieking kid?

That kid now renewed its hollering with a particularly high note that caused him to want to rip out his ears.

Coyotes were beginning to sound better by the minute.

Chapter Sixteen

Before they reached the staging area, Valerie spoke. "I'm thinking."

"Tell me," Guy said, his voice threaded with steel.

"If Phillip wants to give Etta a baby, he'd have to be circling closer to her, wouldn't he?"

Guy was silent for all of two seconds. "That's brilliant, Val. Why didn't I think of that?"

"Probably because you're so worried about Lizzie."

"Like you aren't?"

Valerie saw his hands tighten around the steering wheel, his knuckles turning white. It'd be a wonder if he didn't leave depressions in that wheel.

Valerie's heart was shredding even more than it already had. A man who was like a grenade waiting for someone to pull the pin? She shuddered, thinking of little Lizzie in his hands.

She spoke again. "We'll have to be very careful if we start to close in on him."

"No kidding."

Because that man, if he felt he were losing his last

hope of getting Etta back by way of a child, might do anything. Become like a cornered animal. What might he do to Lizzie then? "Why would he want Etta back?"

"Because he's missing his punching bag? Because he's missing his docile little caretaker? Because he wants total power over someone? Hell, I don't know. I never know what makes people like him tick."

Nor did Valerie. They had all kinds of excuses, these abusive people. Bottom line, it was always someone else's fault that they lost control. They'd *had* to do it.

She'd heard that excuse from murderers, too. They hadn't *meant* to kill. It wasn't *their* fault. Of course, she'd met those with another kind of excuse, too. *Someone told me to do it. I was afraid not to do what I was told.*

Rarely did you get one who'd admit he got his jollies from the power over life and death. That it was a high for them. Most of them were braggarts, proud of themselves. Many of that type bragged to too many friends, giving the cops a prime suspect.

She shook her head, realizing she was wandering useless corridors in her mind. Trying not to think about what could happen to Lizzie in the hands of someone like Phillip Margolis.

It was just too much.

When they reached the staging ground again, searchers were beginning to regather. Valerie wouldn't have blamed them for calling it a day, not in that constant rain with the deep chill it brought along. They sure looked a lot more tired than early that morning and were guzzling coffee from white foam cups.

A tarp had been erected over the coffee urns and a long table. Someone had hauled in more boxes of dried foods. Getting ready for another round.

Guy pulled out the terrain maps again, spreading them on the table, this time looking at the area around the Margolis house. He pored over them with the aid of a bright lantern. Valerie looked closely as well, trying to sort it all out herself.

Guy put his thumb on the map. "This is the Margolis house, right about here. Now we've got to consider Phillip might be circling in on it. But how far out would he go first?"

He raised his head, clearly thinking. "To the east, Gray Cloud said. But that was earlier. Assuming the elder was right, what would that tell us about where he's traveling? He's already come quite a distance from the Chamberlain house. If he's slowly closing in…" Guy bent to the map again.

Valerie spoke. "The Chamberlain house is where?"

Guy stabbed at it.

"And the cabin?"

Again his thumb pointed. "Here."

"And the ATV?"

She looked at him and saw his eyes widen a shade. He traced the map from May's house to the cabin then to the general area Gray Cloud had said was to the east. Then to the abandoned ATV. Which put that area north of the Margolis place. "To the east all right, but a big circle, far from a direct line to his house."

Then he lifted his head. "You did it, Val."

She guessed she had. Somehow.

Guy spoke. "I've got a plan."

That was the best thing she'd heard all day.

IT WAS AN hour or more before searchers headed out. They fueled up first. Some departed from the group apologetically, but livestock needed tending no matter what. Others began to trail in from their morning searches, having gotten so far out.

But new searchers had arrived, too, and hearing Guy's plan they were eager to get going. Again the search areas were sectioned, but everyone got the same message. "You see anything, report it, but don't try to get close to the guy. We don't want him to feel cornered."

And then what? Val wondered, chewing her lip until it started to feel sore.

Guy surprised her by reaching out and touching her lip lightly. "You're going to shred yourself. Find a different nervous habit."

His touch was welcome and despite everything she had to smile faintly. Somehow he always managed to drag her out of the pit, just a little. He had a gift for that.

"This is awful," she said needlessly.

"Just remind yourself of all the times you've had to wait for reports to come in from the streets, from door-knocking. That's what this is."

"Obviously it feels different."

"No shock there."

More thunder boomed hollowly. People were risking lightning strikes out there, risking their necks in more ways than one in this storm. Valerie rubbed her neck, trying to ease the tension that made it ache. "Why did we have to get a storm?"

"Ask the mountain," Guy said with a shrug. "It makes its own weather, like a lot of mountains."

She turned toward him. "Can you hear it?"

"Hear it speak, you mean?"

Valerie nodded.

"When I was a kid, I thought so a few times. Didn't know if I imagined it and haven't heard it since so maybe I did."

She hesitated. "Maybe you shut it down."

He snorted. "I had a lot of more important things on my mind at the time, it's true. Besides, I never had the makings of a medicine man."

Whatever that meant, Valerie thought, but didn't want to probe into places she might not be welcome. She didn't want to do a single thing that might make Guy uncomfortable. He was an admirable man in so many ways.

The chill was beginning to reach through her clothes so she took a package of beef jerky. A good way to chew off anxiety while fueling her body. And it *did* need fuel. "What's that?" she asked, pointing to a paper-wrapped package.

"Deer jerky. You should try it."

"I accept beef as part of the food chain. I haven't quite gotten to deer."

That pulled a short laugh from him. "Deer look cute, don't they? But they sure can be nasty if they get afraid or annoyed. It's like a horse. You don't want to be at the back end if something scares it." Then he shrugged. "We're blessed with all kinds of food, we're grateful for it, and never take more than we'll eat, at least not directly from nature. I won't say anything about packaged foods."

That tugged another small smile from her. "They get on the reservation, too, huh?"

"Hell yeah. We're not saints and no way can we make a Cheeto. Like everyone else, we got polluted." He winked. "Just normal folk."

Mostly, she thought. Except for people like Gray Cloud. Then she remembered Pastor Molly's story.

Okay, then. Just like everyone else on this planet. *Her* world was sure full of people who thought they had a direct line to the Almighty. Or at least claimed to.

"I'd like to know more," she said to Guy.

"Maybe another time. When all this is settled. Then we'll see."

Except that she'd be on her way back to Gunnison, leaving behind what she had begun to think could be a marvelous journey.

Leaving Guy behind.

GRAY CLOUD RETURNED ALONE, water dripping from his oilskins. "He's still out there," he said to Guy. "Hasn't moved. Keep looking."

"Got a pinpoint on him?"

Gray Cloud shook his head, looking surprisingly wry. "Little is given, much has to be learned, usually the hard way." Then he rode away.

Valerie sighed. "Not helpful."

"You're wrong," Guy answered flatly. "He just told us the guy isn't moving. And he didn't say anything about Lizzie. She isn't dead."

"How can you know that?" she demanded, once again on the edge of screaming. "You can't *know* that!"

He regarded her stolidly. "He'd have known if she wasn't."

Valerie walked away, hardly noticing that the rain was beginning to let up.

Nothing. Every damn move in this hunt turned up nothing. What the hell good did it do to believe that Phillip Margolis was behind this? It didn't get them anywhere.

They still had to *find* that bastard.

GUY WATCHED HER walk away. He'd have given his life to put Lizzie into her arms, into May's arms. But they still needed to find her, to find Margolis. There was an awful lot of land out there. Too much, maybe.

He rubbed his brow and adjusted his Stetson. Wearing his uniform sure wasn't greasing the wheels on any of this. Except for Gray Cloud. He wondered if the elder would have come forward with what he heard in the thunder if Guy hadn't been leading this hunt.

Or maybe he would have, despite expecting to be dismissed or thought crazy. Gray Cloud cherished life, all life. He'd have done what he could have, even risking scorn. Guy knew him well enough to believe that.

The rain was lessening, but that wouldn't change the conditions out there for the search parties. The land was a mire protected only by brush and wild grasses that might ease their movement. Maybe.

It was his turn to pray, and he prayed to all the gods he'd ever heard of. The One God.

Inevitably he remembered what Pastor Molly had said. *Who are we to limit the Almighty?*

He decided that he might make an effort to get to know the pastor better. To discover more about that woman and her broader beliefs.

He might like her a whole lot.

But then his thoughts returned to Lizzie. Of all the people to have taken her... Phillip Margolis. A monster.

PHILLIP MARGOLIS COULDN'T stand the crying anymore. He stepped out into the lessening rain to escape. The only thing that ever quieted that brat was riding in the truck. As if it somehow soothed her. The only thing that did. He had to get out of here.

But the idea of taking the truck and moving right then proved impossible. The sod hut had kept out the rain, but when he stepped out he saw the small rivers running downhill along the side of it.

His truck would just get mired. He cussed. He swore every ugly word he knew, then cussed them all over again.

And then, out of the blue, came the memory of Etta threatening to shoot him while he slept.

Maybe his plan to get her back was stupider than he thought.

Being stuck here with that kid was a nightmare. The only consolation he had was that no one could know *he* was the one who had taken that screaming kid. He could abandon that brat and head for the hills as soon as the ground dried a bit.

And that didn't sound like the worst idea he'd ever had.

But what about getting that woman back? Etta. She belonged to him. She was his property as he'd proved countless times. She'd do anything he said.

Including coming with him and that kid as far as he wanted to take them, far beyond detection, to a place they weren't known at all.

She might even be able to quiet that squalling. That was what mothers did, wasn't it?

He stomped down on his own frenzy. He had to get to Etta as soon as possible. Had to get them all away from Conard County. Soon.

If only the ground would dry enough that his truck wouldn't get stuck in mud. Getting stuck would be enough to make him want to kill.

VALERIE RETURNED FROM the mist, walking straight toward Guy. Some of the searchers were returning, carrying bad news about the sogginess of the terrain. Some of the ATVs were finding it impossible to continue. Another strike against this whole idea.

Guy turned from the men and women he was talking to and looked at Valerie. "You gonna be okay?"

"I don't even know what okay is anymore. I need to do something, Guy. Sitting around like this isn't helping. I've got to *act*."

He understood. He wasn't far from feeling the same way himself. "But how?" he asked reasonably. "You're just one person, and if you join the search how much will you add?"

"How can you be so calm?" she demanded.

"Because someone has to be. Someone needs to oversee all this." He balled his fists. "Someone, Val. You know that."

She looked away, giving herself a little shake. "I still need to do more than sit around waiting for news."

He drew a long breath and expelled it between his lips. "You got an idea?"

"I'll go to Etta's place. Wait *there*. He has to come eventually."

"You might be spotted by Margolis."

She shook her head. "If I am, he won't know who I am. Most people don't know yet that I'm a cop. I haven't been around long enough. Anyway, I'd be surprised if the grapevine traveled to Etta. She's as isolated as anyone I've ever seen."

He couldn't argue against that, especially considering that Etta hadn't even known about the kidnapping. "I warned you about Margolis. He's unpredictable and dangerous. You should be armed."

She pulled back the left side of her jacket, revealing her waist holster. "I have my service pistol. But if you think I'm going to shoot anywhere near Lizzie, you couldn't be more mistaken. I'll find another way to deal with him."

Guy reluctantly nodded, completely unhappy with her decision but knowing there was probably no way to stop her. "You can't go alone."

"What, am I going to drive up to that house in your official vehicle? Make a grand appearance that'll keep him away if he's anywhere in sight?"

"Then how are you going to get there?"

She looked around, waving her hand at all the pickups scattered around. "I'll borrow a vehicle."

Guy thought about it for little more than a split second. "I'm going with you. I won't go in the house, though. I'll wait somewhere out of the way in case he shows up. Promise me one thing, though. You'll arrange for Etta to get Lizzie out of his arms before he knows you're there."

She nodded. "Fair enough. I thought about that, but I still won't go in a cop car."

She was right, of course. He considered the problem for a minute or so, then keyed his radio. Static answered him, so he reached for the satellite phone.

"Joe?" he said. "Cal?"

"Yo," came an answer from Joe.

"Can you lend me your truck?"

The answer was prompt. "Keys are still in the ignition. Help yourself."

"Thanks. I take it you haven't seen anything else?"

"One of our group seems to remember an old sod hut about three miles from here. We're closing in on it. Carefully, like you said."

Guy stepped inside the command trailer and looked at the maps on the video screen. "I see you."

"Then come on down if'n you want."

Guy disconnected the call and emerged from the trailer to find Valerie looking sodden and forlorn. She sure as hell couldn't ride a horse. She was still moving gingerly.

He told her what Joe had said.

"Maybe," she answered, "we ought to go to that hut."

"Maybe. But what if he's already moved again? What if he sees us coming?" He knew he kept throwing up roadblocks but he had to consider every possibility.

She chewed her lip again, staring out into the deepening dusk. "It's got to be the Margolis house then. He *does* want to bring Lizzie to Etta."

As good an answer as any. He turned operations over to Artie Jackson and Mark Alton, both adequately experienced to take over now.

"I'll keep in contact," Guy told them, "but at some point I'm going to have to go dark. Don't worry, but I can't risk the sound of a radio or phone."

Then he joined Valerie at Joe's truck, a crew cab in silvery gray, with high suspension and four-wheel drive. It looked as battered as any working truck out here.

"You're going to freeze to death," was all he said to Valerie as they drove away. As soon as he could he turned the truck's heater to high. The blast felt good to his own cold skin. To hers, too, he imagined.

"I didn't exactly come dressed for a downpour," she answered. Nor did she sound as if she cared.

THE JOLTING OF the truck over the bad roads reminded Valerie that she still hadn't recovered from her trip on horseback. Pawing in her pocket, she found the small bottle of ibuprofen and swallowed the pills dry. This truck didn't have soft suspension, and each jolt reminded her of her overworked muscles, some of which she probably hadn't used enough over recent years.

"I need to find time to get back to the gym," she remarked, again trying to distract herself even as her nerves ratcheted up.

"I don't know how much that would help saddle-soreness."

Maybe nothing could, except riding for hours nearly every day. "I feel like a wimp."

"That's the last thing I'd call you."

Small comfort.

SHE TOOK AN opportunity to call May. Guy listened, wishing he could help as he heard Val's side of the conversation.

"Everybody's out looking," Valerie said to May. "Damn near the whole county, as far as I can tell. It's amazing, May."

A pause. Then, "We think we might be closing in on the kidnapper. But I can't be sure. Still, the guy seems to be taking care of Lizzie. Count on that, May. I'll let you know as soon as we have anything."

As unsatisfactory a call as Guy could imagine, but a few scraps for May to cling to. That woman *needed* to cling to hope.

"How's she doing?" Guy asked when Valerie disconnected.

"About as well as anyone could, I guess. She's still breathing, anyway."

"And Chet?"

"Somehow he's managed to be there most of the day. I guess the Conard County birth rate has temporarily dropped."

Guy heard a touch of bitterness in her voice. "Big problem, huh?"

"Not until Lizzie came. Not until May quit her teaching job to become a full-time mother."

"That'd be a heck of a change."

"Too much, I guess. I read that some men get resentful because they're no longer the center of attention for their wives. I don't know for sure because I didn't get Chet's side of the divorce. Not really."

"Some men need to grow up," Guy said sharply.

"Yeah."

He allowed the silence to dominate, along with the *thwap* of the windshield wipers and the creaks from a truck that was getting old from rough use. Eventually he tried to distract her again. Little else he could do.

He spoke. "I guess you study up on human psychology."

"Like Gray Cloud said, some of it we learn the hard way. But yeah, I'm kind of a student."

"Me, too. Always looking for answers for why people behave the way they do."

"Biggest mystery of the universe, as mysterious as black holes and the big bang."

"Those are two things that blow my mind."

She answered with surprising wryness, given the circumstances. "Seems physicists and cosmologists would agree with you."

Another window into this woman, one he liked. They read the same things, were fascinated by the same things. Another link. One he wasn't at all sure he wanted.

THEY REACHED THE Margolis homestead. Rain still fell dismally, although much more lightly. Valerie climbed out and walked to the front door. As soon as Etta opened it and let her in, Guy drove away. She had no idea where he was going but was certain he'd do the wisest thing. She trusted his experience and knowhow. Maybe more than she trusted her own.

Etta was surprisingly glad to see her.

"I didn't want to sit here alone," Etta said. "Not all alone and waiting for Phillip. God knows what he'll do to me. Or that baby. Let me make coffee and soup. You look cold to the bone."

Valerie noticed that the shotgun now stood beside the door. Ready. A change seemed to have come over Etta, too. She no longer looked as shrunken, as hopeless. Maybe she was looking forward to putting two loads of birdshot into her husband.

That wouldn't be surprising.

Etta soon served her hot coffee and a big bowl of canned chicken soup.

"I can't thank you enough for this," Valerie told her.

"Least I can do. I'm grateful you came. Because he's coming. I feel it in my bones. That man would never let me go. I shoulda known that a couple of years wasn't enough for him to get the message."

Etta faced her across the battered kitchen table. "Those deputies didn't find much in the compost heap. Didn't think they would. I buried the damn stuff good."

"How come?"

"Because I was pissed. Crawling back like the slime he is. A snake, although maybe that ain't fair to snakes. Somehow I knew he'd never let go. I was just beginning to hope."

God, this woman still had some fire in her. It was almost as if these events had awakened her from despair.

Valerie's phone rang and she pulled it out of her pocket. Guy.

"I'm in position, Val," he said. "I'm going dark now."

"That's a good idea," Valerie answered. "I'll do that, too."

"Just remember, this puts you on your own."

"I'm not alone. Etta's locked and loaded and ready to shoot."

Guy's laugh was genuine but brief. "Give that woman kudos for me."

Val disconnected and turned her phone off. "Guy's out there. Ready. He said to give you props."

Etta smiled faintly. "Nothin' I ain't wanted to do for years. Just get that little girl away from him, then look out."

Valerie reached across the table, covering Etta's cold, bony hand with her own. "Not unless there's no other choice, Etta. You don't want to go to jail."

"I been in jail most of my grown life. At least in jail I wouldn't be worrying about *him*."

GUY HAD DRIVEN up the road until he'd found a short turnout that ended in barred fence facing a cattle chute. The chute would guide livestock straight into the back of a waiting truck.

He checked his GPS, recalled the terrain map from memory and set out at a slow jog. He had a good idea of where he needed to go.

Finally he hunkered down behind a low hillock that gave him a view of the Margolis house through his night vision goggles. Here he felt no one would be able to come up from behind him without him knowing first. Soggy as the ground was it might deaden footsteps, but on high alert he was sure he wouldn't miss the smallest sound.

Considering the problem, though, he decided that Phillip Margolis would have to come by truck. He couldn't possibly intend to slog his way over so much open ground with Lizzie in his arms. Besides, he'd need his vehicle, whatever it was, to make a quick escape.

He had little doubt that Phillip intended to abscond with both the little girl and his wife. Not if he meant what was in his note.

Nope. Margolis intended to make a clean getaway with them.

He wondered if the cordon was closing in tightly enough to worry Margolis. If he'd caught wind of the search. That might complicate everything. Might put Lizzie in greater danger.

Hell and damnation.

THE WAIT WAS no easier at the house, Valerie thought. Nerves crawled along her skin. This might conceivably take days, especially the way the weather had been today.

Etta seemed okay with the waiting. Naturally she was. She didn't want to see that man again in this lifetime.

"Remember," she said more than once to Etta, "you want to pretend you're happy about the baby. Take Lizzie from his arms. Can you do that?" The question seriously worried her. Most people were lousy actors.

"'Course I can," Etta answered. "Been pretending with that man for a long time. Could never let him see nothin' but fear. He never guessed how I really felt, not until I said I'd shoot him."

Then this might work, Valerie thought. It might. "He can't know I'm here."

"You don't have to tell me that. Get the baby, then you take care of him. I hope you shoot him."

Valerie surely wanted to. Then they both settled back into the endless wait. Etta dozed on a battered, nearly shredded sofa in the main room. Valerie sat in the dark on a chair in the tiny bedroom. No way could she sleep on it because it was like sitting on hard lumps.

But she didn't want to sleep. Someone had to remain awake.

At least Guy was out there somewhere, although he might not be able to do much from where he was.

But if her plan in this house went awry and Margolis got away with Etta and Lizzie, Guy would take care of it.

With that, for now, she had to be content.

Except contentment was not part of her basic mood. No, she kept thinking about Guy in ways that felt awful in the present circumstances. How could she let desire run through her *now*?

She had Lizzie to worry about. So why was she thinking about a tall, strong man with an unmistakable Indigenous face, a man in whom she sensed a deep-rooted anger? Why was she thinking about how sexy he was, how fascinating?

About how much better she wanted to know him.

She ought to feel disgusted with herself under these circumstances, but disgust refused to come.

All she felt was a longing, a yearning. One that could never amount to anything. Not when she had to leave. Not when he had every right to scorn her world.

And, by extension, to scorn her.

God, she was a flaming mess.

THE STORM HAD PASSED. Phillip Margolis stepped outside the tiny hut. At least the brat had fallen asleep, the only escape he got. This was a stupid idea. He wanted to kick his own butt.

At least the ground felt firmer now. The little rivers were slowing down as they passed the hut. Soon he'd dare to move. Probably not until late tomorrow when night might provide some cover.

Not that he expected anyone to be interested in his place. No reason. They didn't know about him.

The moon peeked between scudding clouds, giving him some light to see by. Dawn was almost here.

He turned around to go back inside when he caught sight of movement atop a nearby hill.

His heart nearly stopped. Two men on horseback. Were they hunting for him? He swore under his breath. What now? He was sure he'd left no trail.

But then the two men turned their mounts away, disappearing behind the hill.

Margolis began to breathe again. Just a couple of cowboys checking out the range after the storm. That was all they could be. Because no one on this damn planet could know *he'd* taken the kid. Or where he was hanging out.

No one. He'd made damn sure of that.

But once again he thought about leaving that kid behind and just getting out of here.

Then he thought about Etta. He wanted that woman back where she belonged, and the brat was the price of taking her back.

She'd want the kid. Of course she would. After they'd lost their own, she'd never stopped sniveling no matter how many times he hit her. That had been almost as infuriating as that kid inside the hut.

Settled in his own mind, he went back inside to enjoy a little quiet. He'd have liked a fire, but that was too dangerous, smoke coming out of an abandoned hut.

He was too smart to make that mistake. Then he decided he was a pretty smart man.

There was no way on earth that they knew who had taken the kid, and they had no way to find him.

Satisfied, he even let himself sleep in an ancient chair. The silence from the brat was a relief.

Chapter Seventeen

Morning's gray light began to glow dimly in the east. Guy rubbed his eyes to clear the grit out of them, then returned to watching the house.

Soon the sky grew brighter, a crystalline light purified by yesterday's storm. Probably pretty, but he was in no mood to notice. The night's cold and damp had made him ache a bit, and he longed to stand up and move around, but didn't dare for fear of being spotted.

Instead he had to work on squirming a limb at a time. It wasn't enough, but it had to do, at least until the sun began to warm him.

He wished he dared turn on his radio, to see if he could get any news, but if Margolis was anywhere nearby that would be as stupid as standing up in case he heard it. He trusted his people, but even trust had its limits when you hungered for information.

He wondered about Valerie, about how miserable she must be as well. He doubted she'd slept any better than he had. Something had to happen soon or they'd both become useless.

But given all the empty time, all the time when his immediate concerns weren't enough, he thought about Valerie in a different way.

She was beautiful. No question. But she was more than just a sexy woman. A confident, experienced cop. A woman full of a determination that he admired. A woman who shared some of his own interests.

A woman who'd found a way to cross a threshold that was important to him. She'd found a way to believe Gray Cloud.

But was that enough?

He reminded himself that once this case concluded she'd head back to Gunnison. No reason for her to stay here.

So maybe it was okay to while the time by having thoughts he shouldn't be having. Neither of them would be in danger from *that*.

But she was still a woman he wanted to hold close. To cradle in his arms. To claim with both his mind and body. He remembered as if it were etched into his mind the one time he'd held her to comfort her. Not the same at all, but his body kept wanting to remember anyway.

Had he ever felt this way before? He couldn't say he had. Not like this. Not even with his first girlfriend so long ago. Indigenous like himself, making her a much wiser choice, a woman who shared his culture.

But she hadn't drawn him the way Val did.

Hell's bells.

THE HOURS CONTINUED to drag. The perfectly blue sky seemed to sneer at Valerie. She wanted to step outside and look around but knew that wouldn't be sensible. Her tension, already bad enough, rose even more.

Worse, now that she wasn't at the staging area, she'd give almost anything to know what was happening there. News of any kind?

Instead she shared a breakfast of stale cereal and coffee with Etta.

"I eat it without milk," Etta said apologetically. "I don't get to town often and milk spoils too fast. That Pastor Molly takes care of a lot for me. She brings me bags of groceries when she can. A few times she took me to the store. She's a good woman."

"The cereal's okay," Val answered. "It tastes good anyway." She was hungry enough to think *hay* would taste good right now. "So you get television out here?" She pointed to the ancient tube TV on its stand across the room.

"Satellite," Etta answered. "Since Phillip left I ain't been able to adjust it, though. Picture's getting snowy."

"Maybe after all this is done I can get somebody to fix it for you."

Etta nodded. "Sure would be nice. I used to have a kitchen garden. When I was out there working on it…well, that was the only time Phillip left me alone. He liked them fresh veggies, too. So I could be out there and for a little while I could be safe."

Valerie's heart squeezed. "But you don't do it anymore?"

Etta shrugged. "Too hard for me to keep up the compost pile. Needed Phillip to turn it over with the pitchfork. But I still throw scraps on it anyway. Habit, I s'pose."

Etta stared off into space and Valerie wondered what she was thinking about. She didn't feel she could ask, though. Etta's thoughts were her own, and Valerie had no right to pry.

Etta scooped up the cereal bowls and put them in the sink. Then she poured more coffee. "I'm gonna be leavin' soon."

Val drew a sharp breath. "Why?" Her mind was already scrambling, dredging up awful ideas.

"Cuz I can't to keep the place up. Ran out of money a while ago so I don't do the repairs. The rancher who owns it, Mr. Dawson, all he asked was for us to keep up the place. One of these days he's gonna notice I ain't doing it. He'll be wanting to get some other folks in here."

"But where will you go? What will you do?"

Etta shrugged. "Don't make no mind."

But it *did* matter, Valerie thought. This woman had reached the end of her rope in every way possible. If she hadn't been so worried about Lizzie, she'd worry a whole lot about what was going to happen to Etta Margolis. Her life appeared to be on a permanent downward spiral.

"I wish that man would get here," Etta said angrily. "I want this over. I want *him* over."

"Me, too, Etta."

The woman eyed her. "Bet you do. As much as me. She's your niece, huh?"

"She is."

"Then maybe you ought to shoot him more'n once."

"Don't tempt me."

MARGOLIS WOULDN'T BE traveling on foot across rough ground with Lizzie. Not unless he'd tipped over his own mental edge.

Guy knew that in his bones. However the man approached, he was going to need to do it in his vehicle. Whether he drove by road or over land made no difference. Unless he left Lizzie behind for some reason.

Like he wanted to get rid of the little girl. A band clamped around Guy's chest. Or maybe the guy would want to scout first. Also a possibility.

But there was no reason for Phillip Margolis to suspect they knew he was the kidnapper. Maybe he'd drive up to Etta's door bold as you please.

Finally, as the day's breeze woke in the sun's heat, he dared to turn on his radio and contact the operation trailer. The voice that answered was Gage Dalton's, to Guy's surprise. Apparently the sheriff couldn't sit this one out at his desk.

"How's it going?" Gage asked without preamble.

"Nothing yet."

"Same here, so far. The cordon you set is tightening around the Margolis house. Reckon he's got to move soon. He's been getting closer."

"He *was* getting closer. Now we don't know. Has

anyone seen that sod hut someone thought they re-called yesterday?" Not that he had much hope it'd be easy to find a sod hut. After a hundred and fifty years, grasses and brush would have grown on it, concealing it.

"Not a peep," Gage replied. "Valerie still in the house with Etta?"

"Yup."

"Good. Just let me know if you want eyes in the sky."

Oh, man, would he like a helicopter searching out there. "I don't want to scare him, Gage. He might do something to Lizzie. You know what Margolis is like."

Gage's sigh was audible over the airwaves. "Too much risk at this point," he agreed finally. "Hard to be so close yet so far."

"Tell me about it. I'm going dark again."

Then he switched off the radio and took another scan of the area through his binoculars. No sign of any vehicle. No sign of anyone crossing the open ground.

Guy was getting tired of the sound of his own smothered cussing. Nothing creative or helpful there.

Nothing helpful from the heavens either. Just so deep, clear and blue that it hurt his eyes to look up at it.

Regardless, Guy rolled on his back to stare up into it anyway and pulled a piece of deer jerky from his pocket. His jaws ached as he chewed it.

Well, hell, what *didn't* ache? His heart sure did.

VALERIE TRIED TO practice some deep breathing and muscle relaxation, almost like meditation, but she was having trouble keeping at it.

She kept eyeing that shotgun beside the front door. It would be too deadly in this confined space. It would spread its load everywhere, endangering everyone. She wondered if she should conceal it somewhere and rely on her own semiautomatic.

But removing that gun might scare Etta. She obviously felt a strong need to be able to protect herself from her husband. Facing him filled her at once with terror and a strong urge to kill him.

What if she didn't take Lizzie away from Phillip? What if she just reacted to her own instinct to kill that bastard?

So once again she reiterated the plan to Etta, who managed a scornful look.

"You think I'm stupid? I want to kill that man but I don't want to kill no baby. Gotta be able to live with myself, even if it's in jail for the rest of my livelong days."

Valerie appreciated the sentiment. She'd spend the rest of her life in jail, too, if it meant taking out that SOB. Pay him back for all he'd done to Lizzie and May. Never before had she felt such a strong murderous urge. She'd always relied on the law to take care of the monsters, even if it never seemed like enough payback.

But she'd had to face the fact, a long time ago, that these monsters were human, too. Not another species. Just one of the worst expressions of the human race. Perfectly human, in other words.

But like most people, she still thought of them as monsters. Other than human. Still, it was no excuse for the rest of the people who occupied this planet. Some crimes were heinous, but that didn't mean others weren't capable of them.

That ugliness dwelt in everyone, rarely evoked, rarely acted upon. Just look at her right now. She wanted to kill and hoped she'd find some justification if the chance arose.

Feeling a whole load of self-disgust, she walked from window to window, standing far enough back that she wouldn't show through the glass.

What was happening out there? What was Guy doing?

Guy was belly-crawling closer to the house. He'd decided to get into a better range to act when Margolis showed up. Needing a place where he couldn't be seen through one of those windows.

He felt some self-disgust, too. He'd fallen asleep on watch. Not for long. Probably eased by the conviction he'd hear any kind of motor approach.

No excuse anyway, even though the nap had freshened his mind, made him feel stronger. The only part of this he really hated was that he was probably leaving a clear trail in the soggy ground behind him. Giving himself away if Margolis happened along here in his truck.

He didn't want the man to hightail it.

But there was always the chopper. Even if Margolis tried to run, they'd be able to follow him. Small comfort.

And Lizzie? Tossed from a moving vehicle to cover the crime?

Guy's stomach churned then settled into a tight, leaden knot. He felt hamstrung.

MAY HAD BEGUN to feel even more frantic. No word from Val since yesterday. No news from the police except they thought they were closing in.

How could they be sure of that? How could anyone? Then one of the people who again started filling her house turned on the TV. As soon as she saw the bulletin about Phillip Margolis, she knew. Knew with absolute certainty.

"I'm going out to his house," she announced.

More than one of her friends said she couldn't.

She glared at them. "Are you going to stop me? How?" Into her panic, into her determination, came one calm voice.

"May?" said Pastor Molly. "May, you shouldn't do that."

"Why the hell not?"

"Because you might interfere with the police operation."

May shook her head. "What operation? They haven't found her yet."

Molly nodded to the TV. "Now they know who they're looking for. Trust them to take care of it. Trust your sister."

"Oh, God," May wailed. "Trust? I don't trust anyone at all!"

The people around her froze.

Molly approached her and took her into a gentle hug. "Yes, you do. You trust Val."

At last May started to sag against Molly. "I've got to do *something*!"

"But you don't want to risk getting in the way. To risk complicating things by involving yourself. They've got enough to worry about with Lizzie and that man. They don't need to be worrying about you, too."

JUST THEN, CHET walked into the house, his eyes seeking May.

May straightened, pulling away from Molly. "This is all *your* fault. All of it." Then she stormed away to her bedroom.

Everyone in the room stared at him, apparently agreeing with May. Except for Pastor Molly. At least she didn't offer some anodyne that wouldn't have worked. Clenching and unclenching his fists, he looked from face to face, taking in the silent accusation.

He left, but not before he saw the bulletin on the TV screen. Standing out front under a brilliant sky, trees rustling in the breeze, a memory grabbed him.

Phillip Margolis. Chet remembered that case all too well. The fury he'd endured from Margolis, the threats. The wild grief from Etta. Those godawful moments when he'd had to deliver unthinkable news and then withstand the reaction.

One of the times he wished he hadn't gone into obstetrics. One of the many times he'd been sure it wasn't his fault. Not that the knowledge helped him deal with their pain, or his own.

His fists clenched again as he stared into the past.

He wasn't at all sure that May wasn't right. Maybe it *was* all his fault.

PHILLIP MARGOLIS WAS getting far past the end of his tether. The brat was screaming again. She spat out the mashed peas he tried to give her.

He changed a stinky diaper again, a diaper that was stinkier that the first ones, trying to ignore the crying that drilled into his brain.

Even his inexperienced eyes could tell the kid was losing weight.

Damnation. He had to get this kid to Etta or he wouldn't get a chance with her. What if the kid was sick and died? Then what?

His aching head couldn't think about the *and then*.

Go! his brain was shrieking. *Get the kid out of here and to Etta. Make* her *take care of this*.

Riding in the truck always made the brat shut up. Always put her to sleep. Besides, nobody'd be looking for *him*. He could just drive up to his own front door. Which maybe he should have done first thing except he'd been afraid of leaving a trail. No, he wanted to be sure no one was on his tail.

Desperate, he stepped outside and looked around.

No one in sight. He checked the firming ground and made up his mind.

Running around to the back of the hut, he pulled the clay-stiffened brown tarp from the old pickup. Rusty and ancient, it ran good, which was the whole reason he'd stolen it from a scrap yard. Perfectly good engine in there, with a little tweaking.

Four more miles and he could dump the kid on Etta, who'd get what she'd always wanted. A baby. A squalling brat. A pain in the head and neck. She could take care of it and him, too.

She'd get that crying to stop.

Then he went back around front and saw the kid halfway out the front door.

He should have gotten one that couldn't walk yet. But Chet Chamberlain didn't have a slew to pick from.

He grabbed the kid, wrapped it in a filthy blanket then went around to stuff her in the truck. For some reason he suddenly recalled the baby seat that had been given to them by the sheriff's department. A freebie, coming with a bunch of instruction and warnings about how it was important to use it for the child's safety. How thrilled Etta had been with it, how often she had touched it. Then he shrugged it off and put the struggling bundle on the truck's floor in front of the ratty passenger seat.

Chamberlain deserved everything he got. Then Margolis looked at the drying ground again.

Now or never.

Chapter Eighteen

Now that midday approached and with it the breezy sounds that would help cover the radio, Guy checked in again. Gage was still out there at the operations trailer.

"One of the searchers spied a truck headed south on the county road in the direction of the Margolis place. Moving slow."

Adrenaline hit Guy like a punch. "We're ready." He wished he could give Val a heads-up, but she was still dark. No sounds that might warn anyone. Because she had no way of knowing for sure that Margolis wouldn't come on foot.

Guy was sure now. He disconnected, turned off the phone, going dark again.

But now he had a direction to guide him. The bastard was going to pull up to his own front door, deluded into thinking that no one was looking for him.

Guy prayed that Lizzie was with Margolis. That he hadn't left the little girl somewhere to draw Etta out.

Hell if he'd let Margolis leave unwatched. If the

guy didn't carry a kid into that house, then it would be time for the chopper. Or to get someone to follow Margolis to wherever he went with Etta.

Guy swore again, aware of how many ways this could all go wrong. How many ways Lizzie's life could be risked. How many bad things might happen.

But some decisions had to wait until he knew if Margolis had the child with him.

He belly-crawled closer to the house, to a place where he could step in if he had to.

At this point he'd have put a gun to Margolis's head if necessary to find out where Lizzie was.

If there was one thing he knew about Margolis's type of bully it was that they were all cowards at heart.

AT THE CHAMBERLAIN HOUSE, May emerged from her bedroom to all the kindly faces that waited for her. They all meant well, but she was past caring about it. Other than getting Lizzie back, she wanted just one thing.

"Where's Chet?" she asked.

"He left," Janine Baxter said.

May's face, all swollen from crying more tears that she would have ever believed anyone could shed, said, "It's not his fault."

Janine replied, "It's Chet who needs to hear that, not us."

STILL STANDING OUTSIDE, hating his helplessness, hating himself, Chet squeezed his eyes shut. There was only one baby he wanted to hold in his hands right now. Just one.

His phone rang and he automatically answered it.

His office assistant was calling. "Mary Pringle is on her way to the hospital."

Another delivery. He couldn't deal with that right now. "Tell Lucy to take it. She can fit it in somehow. I can't... Not right now."

"She'll understand."

"She damn well ought to." He'd been making all kinds of excuses for Lucy because she had a young family. He was through. He'd made excuses for her when he had his *own* family to care for. He'd failed.

What had made him do that? A sense of responsibility to his patients? Or a need for control? After this, if there was an *after* worth living for, he needed to deal with himself.

Then, stunning him, he heard May call him. Wondering if he was hallucinating, he turned slowly and saw her standing in the doorway.

"Chet," she said, her voice wobbly. "I was wrong. I need you."

With no reluctance whatsoever, he walked toward her.

PHILLIP MARGOLIS TOOLED down the road slowly, mainly because the kid had shut up. The minute he stopped, that little brat would start up again. He needed some time to prepare for shrieking, even if he meant to dump the kid on Etta.

But God, he was enjoying the quiet. Nothing

but the rumble of an engine and the creaking of the truck's aging frame.

Yeah, he'd get them far away, because if he didn't someone would notice him and Etta suddenly had a child. He'd make his wife come with him. Easy to do with the kid.

Visions of Denver or Billings filled his worn-out head. Places with things to do. Bars. Living here at the back of beyond, he'd missed going to bars whenever he wanted.

He'd missed a lot of things, he suddenly realized. All because of Etta. All because he couldn't trust her by herself.

His anger at his wife began to surge. Damn woman was to blame for all of this. *All* of it.

As soon as he got her away from here, he would teach her a lesson she'd never forget. Threaten to shoot him? He'd make sure she'd never even think of that again.

Visions of vengeance replaced visions of bigger towns to hide in. Yeah, he'd teach her good.

GUY SWORE AS another rock poked him in the ribs. He'd be black and blue all over when this was done. Not that he cared.

He hoped Val was okay. This wait had to have been harder on her than him. Hunkered down inside that house, unable to do anything at all, with no idea what was happening. If anyone knew where Margolis might be. If they had a hope in hell of rescuing Lizzie soon.

All Guy wanted at this point was to see Margolis in cuffs and Valerie walking into her sister's house to put Lizzie safely in May's arms.

It didn't seem like such a big thing to wish, but it was *huge*.

Etta Margolis was growing increasingly stressed, increasingly afraid.

Valerie slipped her arm around the woman's shoulder. "Just remember you won't be alone with him. I'll be here. You know that. Just get him to give you Lizzie. I'll take care of the rest."

Etta's eyes drifted to the shotgun.

"No, Etta," Valerie said firmly. "You don't want to hurt the baby."

Etta shook her head. "I told you I don't. It's the last thing I want. But then let me plug Phillip. Please."

Valerie squeezed her a bit. "No, Etta. Let the law take him away. We will, I promise. He'll go away for a long, long time."

Etta's pallid face turned to her. "But he'll be getting out someday, won't he?"

Oh, God, Valerie thought. This woman was on a hair trigger. Not fully trustworthy. She took Etta by the shoulders. "Please, help me save my niece, hard as it might be. Please."

Etta squared her shoulders a little. "Yeah. We gotta save your niece. We gotta."

There was still some hope that this woman wouldn't fall apart at the crucial moment. But now

Valerie had another thing to worry about: Etta's state of mind.

Then Etta went to get the shotgun, putting it nearby.

Valerie closed her eyes briefly. That shotgun was Etta's only lifeline. Or at least she perceived it that way.

But if Etta took Lizzie from Phillip, she'd have to abandon that protection. She wouldn't be able to shoot with a child in her arms.

What Valerie had believed might be getting better was steadily getting worse. She struggled for a way to break Etta out of her spiral.

"Do you want to hear about the puppy I rescued on my way up here?"

Slowly Etta's eyes focused on her. "A puppy?"

"Yes. Hit by a car. I found him on the roadside, but he needed surgery. He's getting better now. He also needs a home. Would you like to adopt him?"

"He got a name?"

"Not yet. That's for you to decide, if you want him."

Etta nodded slowly. "Never dared have a dog before. Always wanted one."

"Then let me tell you about this little guy."

GAGE WAITED AT the staging area, following the search. Many of the people had been reeled in as the cordon tightened. Others had been instructed to keep their eyes on the truck without being seen.

And still that truck rolled slowly down the county road. Too slowly as far as Gage was concerned.

Connie popped her head out of the trailer. "Boss?"

He turned, wincing a bit. "Yeah?"

"Two of the guys found the sod hut. Don't know if that's much good now, but they said it's been occupied recently. Food cans, diapers, that kind of thing. Lizzie isn't there, though."

"Good. More evidence. Tell them not to touch a thing."

More evidence? He hoped they didn't need it, that Margolis would pull up at his own front door. It was good, though, that he hadn't abandoned the girl there. All the good Gage could see just then.

He wondered how Valerie Brighton was doing inside that house. If she could trust Etta Margolis to cooperate. And how close Guy might have managed to get.

Three people to depend on, one of whom might not be trustworthy at all.

Waiting was never easy, even though he'd had to do plenty of it in his undercover days with the DEA. Experience didn't help, though. Impatience grew and, along with it, inescapable tension.

VALERIE HEARD THE engine in the distance. She had to tell herself that it could be any vehicle, but her heart raced anyway.

Soon. Very soon.

She sought internal calm, aware that she might

have to deal with Etta, too. Complicating the whole thing.

She looked at Etta. "He may be coming. Remember, Lizzie first."

Etta glared. "You don't haveta keep telling me."

Valerie hoped that was so.

GUY HEARD THE engine, too. He crawled even closer to the house. Adrenaline still spurred him.

Picking up his binoculars, he looked as best he could down the driveway and saw a truck turn in.

This was it. Now just let the man get out of the truck with the baby. Let him take Lizzie inside where Valerie was no doubt ready.

Nearly holding his breath, Guy watched the truck approach. Then he saw Margolis climb out and walk around to the passenger side. The man looked impatient but didn't look around as if he thought he might be observed. Then he reached inside and lifted out a bundle.

The bundle started screaming.

VALERIE, PULLING HER pistol out, said quietly, "I'll be right here, just around this corner." One of the few corners in this house.

Etta gave a tight nod but her hand reached out to caress the butt of the shotgun that stood right beside her.

Valerie felt every muscle in her body tighten with apprehension. If that woman reached for that shotgun, she'd be the first one to go down. The very first.

Then would come a mess beyond description. Margolis would still have Lizzie. Would he try to run or use the little girl as a shield?

Be out there, Guy. Be out there nearby.

GUY WAS OUT THERE, all right. As close as he could get without revealing himself. For the first time he wished he had a rifle. A pistol wasn't nearly as good for aiming. Too easy to miss a target. Too easy to shoot Lizzie.

Not that he wanted to shoot anywhere near the child. He'd far prefer to charge in there like a raging bull.

THE TRUCK STOPPED in front of the house. Valerie heard a car door slam. Then she heard Lizzie start to cry. Still alive. A breath of relief whispered through her.

From where she stood, she could still see Etta but not the front door. Her hand tightened on her pistol grip. She released the safety, held the gun in both hands, barrel down. Ready.

MUCH AS PHILLIP MARGOLIS had come to hate the kid who writhed against him and screamed, he still felt a sense of triumph as he approached the front door.

The latch was still as useless as it had always been, so he simply kicked it open. It wouldn't matter since he planned to leave with Etta and the brat just as soon as he could get her packed and into the truck. He'd never need that damn door again.

He immediately saw Etta in the interior gloom. Saw the shotgun beside her.

"Look what I done brought you, Etta. You don't wanna be hurtin' our kid, do ya?"

Etta, that dried-up woman, shook her head jerkily. "Ours?" she croaked.

"Yeah, a pretty one, too. 'Cept she won't shut up. You can shut her up, Etta. You're the mom now."

He walked toward her, holding Lizzie forward for Etta to embrace. She took an unsteady step toward him. He was more relieved than he wanted to admit when she moved away from the shotgun.

"Is she pretty?" Etta asked, extending her arms.

"Yeah. Really. But you gotta make her stop cryin' or I'm ditchin' her. Up to you."

"I'll take her," Etta said with another unsteady step. "How'd you get me this baby?"

Lizzie was setting up her usual ruckus. Just as soon as he got Etta to take hold of this brat, he was going to tell her to pack. And while he waited he was going to step outside again, just to escape that screaming.

VALERIE HAD TENSED until every single muscle in her body felt like overstretched steel. Her hands held the butt of her pistol as she peered around the corner. She needed Etta to get Lizzie clear of Phillip, but as they met with the baby between them, she clamped her teeth together.

Just get on with the exchange!

OUTSIDE, GUY WATCHED Margolis disappear inside. The sound of Lizzie's shrieking tore at his heart. He moved even closer, getting into a position that would allow him to spring at the first opportunity.

What was going on inside? His heart thudded in his chest like a blacksmith's hammer.

NOW FIRMLY HOLDING the little girl, Etta stepped away from Margolis. "You poor little baby," she murmured. Then, "Damn it, Phillip. You don't know a thing about caring for a child."

"I changed her diapers, didn't I? She won't eat, neither. You take care of that from now on."

Two steps away. Turning her back to Phillip. "I'll just do that now. You got diapers?"

"In the truck. But first you get your own stuff together. We're leaving."

Etta turned around again, rocking the baby. "Where to?" Then she started singing a soft lullaby. Lizzie hiccupped and her cries began to ease.

"Somewhere ain't nobody gonna find us. Somewhere you can raise that damn kid without interference."

"Except you," Etta said sharply, then resumed rocking Lizzie and singing. Another step away.

Valerie tried to judge if the two were now separated enough that she could act before Phillip could grab Etta and Lizzie and turn them into hostages.

One more step, Etta. Please. Just one more step.

GUY WAS AS close as he could get without warning Margolis that he was out here. He wanted to be closer, much closer. But again he had to wait. He figured he must be grinding his teeth to nubs.

FAR ENOUGH, VALERIE DECIDED. And now the quickest way to protect Etta and Lizzie was with her gun.

Sliding around the corner, gun raised in both hands, she saw Phillip Margolis's eyes grow wide.

Then she pulled the trigger. Right in the thigh as she'd wanted. Margolis fell, screaming.

And Valerie didn't care if he bled to death.

AT THE GUNSHOT, Guy vaulted from the ground, onto the front porch and inside. Etta stood holding the baby, her eyes tightly closed. Valerie stood in a marksman's stance, her face white.

Then he looked down at the man lying on the floor, writhing in pain, bleeding heavily. He keyed his radio. "I need an ambulance at the Margolis place. Now. He's been shot."

Without another word, he went to Valerie and gently lowered her hands, taking the gun from her. Then he wrapped her in his arms.

"It's okay, Val," he said. "It's okay now."

A shudder ripped through Valerie. "He needs a tourniquet."

"Like I give a damn."

Unfortunately, given the spurt he saw from Margolis's leg, he knew an artery had been hit. He'd bleed out fast. Hating the world for just an instant, Guy shredded an old sheet to wrap tightly around the guy's upper thigh.

"You should've hit him in the chest," he said to Val.

"Too easy. I want the bastard to suffer."

At last she moved, approaching Etta and taking Lizzie into her arms.

"Lizzie," she said softly, then began to weep.

Chapter Nineteen

Guy stepped out onto the front porch and keyed his radio, reaching Gage. "We've got her. Lizzie seems okay but needs a look-over, maybe the hospital. Tell May. Send two ambulances. Margolis has been shot in the leg."

Then he went back inside to keep an eye on Val. She had to be on a ragged edge, given the past days, the surge of adrenaline that must be draining, given that she had just shot a man. Given that she finally held Lizzie in her arms, apparently safe and sound.

Two ambulances raced up the rutty drive and paramedics jumped out as soon as they stopped. They attended immediately to Margolis, then put him on a stretcher and carried him out.

Through it all, Valerie stood holding Lizzie, tears running down her face. She rocked the baby and finally looked at Etta.

"Thank you."

Etta offered a brief nod, then a smile. "Did my heart good to see that man shot. Too bad you want him alive."

Guy spoke. "Imagine him spending years and years in prison."

Etta's smile widened. "Might go visit him just to enjoy it. Them other prisoners ain't gonna be nice to him."

"Not when they hear he kidnapped a young child. Even the worst of them have limits."

Etta nodded again, then looked at Valerie and Lizzie. "It's a good thing," she said presently. "Best damn thing I ever done in my whole damn life."

THE OTHER TWO paramedics checked Lizzie over head to foot. Valerie didn't want to let go of her niece but knew she had to. All she could do was shake her head as they uncovered the small child and began to examine her.

One looked at Valerie. "She needs to go to the hospital. Some dehydration. A bad diaper rash. Maybe underfed." Then they wrapped the child in a fresh, clean blanket.

Lizzie had grown quiet, unusual for her with strangers. As if she were too weak to cry anymore. Val drew a deep breath, trying to steady herself, fearing for Lizzie in a new way.

She turned her attention to Guy. "Let May know."

"I'm sure she's already getting a call."

She nodded and climbed aboard the ambulance with Lizzie.

GUY WATCHED THEM GO, wishing he could follow, but there was still some cleaning up to do.

He turned to Etta. "We're going to find a way to help you, Etta. Some way to get you out of this ramshackle house and in among people who'll care."

Etta sagged into that rickety kitchen chair looking drained. "Been thinking about leavin' but I been livin' this way too long to change."

"You might be surprised. The sun doesn't have to be only outside. It can be inside, too."

Etta dragged her gaze to him. "And some folks call you a stupid damn redskin." She shook her head, then looked down. "Damn fools everywhere. What do I need 'em for?"

Sometimes Guy wondered that himself.

THE TRIP TO the hospital seemed to take forever, the ambulance jouncing over the rutty road.

"Sorry for the bumpy ride," one paramedic said.

"Like you pave the county roads," Valerie answered.

At last they turned onto smoother pavement. Flashing lights but no siren. No real urgency. That relieved Valerie just a little. She needed assurances from a doctor, treatment for Lizzie.

Lizzie looked so tiny on that huge stretcher. One of the medics was on the radio, describing the situation. Except for dehydration, it didn't sound that awful. Not yet, anyway.

When they arrived at the hospital, she climbed out of the ambulance to make way for the stretcher. The first thing she saw was May and Chet standing just outside the entrance. They both rushed toward the stretcher.

Moments later, Lizzie and her parents were whisked away. Valerie stood alone outside the ER, suddenly aimless. Lizzie didn't need her now, needed only Chet and May. Later she could see her niece.

Right now, Valerie needed something else. Someone else. Someone who'd walked through this fire right at her side.

She turned around, wondering how to get to Guy's apartment. She couldn't remember. She hadn't paid much attention when he'd taken her there. Maybe she could get directions from someone.

Then she saw the Suburban squeal up, lights flashing.

Guy jumped out and came running toward her. A muddy, grassy mess from his night crawling overground.

She didn't care how dirty he was when he wrapped his arms around her. Held her tight.

"You're coming home with me," he said.

It was the only place she wanted to go.

GUY PRACTICALLY MOTHERED VAL. He steadied her up the stairs. Put sugary food in front of her and a sweet cola in her hand. Told her to drink. Got her a blanket when she started to shiver.

Sat beside her, holding her hand. "Drink. Eat. Don't argue with me."

She felt no desire to argue with him. Instead she

obeyed his orders, draining half the cola in one draft. Eating a cinnamon bun as if her life depended on it.

He reached for the same for himself. A short time later he pressed another bun into her hand. "You need the sugar," he reminded her. "But you know that."

Yes, she knew that. After all the adrenaline, she *did* need every sugary morsel. Licking the stickiness off her fingers, she accepted another soft drink.

"I'll be okay," she finally said.

"You will," he agreed. "You're tough. Tough as ten cops."

"I doubt that. *You* were there."

"It wasn't *my* niece."

"She might as well have been. I've been beside you all the way through this. You never cared less than I did."

"Just doing my job."

Right, she thought. *Right*.

AN HOUR LATER, May called. Guy waited while Val talked to her sister, then disconnected.

She looked at Guy, smiling. "Lizzie's okay. She's going to be fine. They want to keep her overnight, though. I can visit once they get her into a regular room."

"Want me to come with?"

"Of course. You did as much as anyone to bring Lizzie home. Then I gotta figure out how to thank most of this county."

"I think the news will be enough."

Val finally sagged into the recliner and fell into a deep sleep.

Good, Guy thought. He took the opportunity for a long, hot shower to wash away the infinite filth that covered him in the last stages of this case. He wished he could as easily shower away the ugliness in his brain. Then he dressed in a fresh uniform.

Still a lot of cleaning up to do with the case. T's to cross and i's to dot. There'd be a whole lot of forensic evidence to review, too. Not that they'd need much after the scene in the Margolis household, but charges other than kidnapping could probably be leveled against Phillip Margolis, too, charges like child abuse. Guy wanted to throw the entire book at that monster.

He wished he'd been the one to shoot Margolis. Val didn't strike him as the type who'd be able to brush it aside. She was the type who'd carry that single shot with her for the rest of her life, no matter how justified it had been. He'd rather carry that burden himself.

He sighed quietly, wiping his face. He saw an Indigenous face in his mirror and he'd always been proud of it, even when others tried to steal that pride.

He brewed a pot of coffee while Val continued to sleep away her exhaustion. Glancing at the clock, he figured it wouldn't be long before Val wanted to go to the hospital.

Reluctantly he carried a mug of coffee toward the recliner, then shook her gently.

She came instantly awake, instantly alert.

"Coffee," he said, handing her the mug. "Then I'm taking you home so you can clean up before we go to the hospital."

She offered him a faint smile. "I guess you already took care of that for yourself."

"Hell, yeah. That damn brush was prickly."

At long last she laughed. "Bet I had an easier night than you did."

"That depends on your perspective."

An old towel in the trunk took care of wiping the dirt and dust from the driver's seat in his vehicle. The outside was splattered with mud. Well, Gage wouldn't like that. All official vehicles were supposed to gleam.

Then he chuckled quietly. As if Gage would care this time.

The end of this long siege was beginning to get to him, too. After all the fear, all the worry that they'd never find Lizzie, after all the effort they'd put out to find the little girl, it had started to sink in that Lizzie was okay, the job was successfully concluded.

Odd, he couldn't remember ever having felt at loose ends before.

He drove Val to the Chamberlain house, then waited outside for her. Unfortunately, that gave him time to think about Val. About how much he'd started to dread the day when she returned to Gunnison. About the hole she'd leave behind in him.

Then he started counting all the reasons he shouldn't feel this way. There were probably a dozen or more, but he stopped at a few. Her job was elsewhere. She wouldn't quit to stay here. He wouldn't want her to either. What would she do here?

He wouldn't quit to follow her. Not that she'd want him to.

Nope, there was that huge cultural and possibly even racial divide. Separate lives intersecting only because of a crisis. He needed to remember that.

Val emerged from the house thirty minutes later, wearing one of those business suits he'd first seen her in. Resuming herself. Resuming her own life.

Maybe sending a message. And maybe he should read it. The hole inside him began to grow.

At the hospital, May and Chet were clearly so happy that they could barely contain their joy. Both of them profusely thanked Valerie and Guy.

"You saved her." May beamed at them. "And, Val, I knew you'd help."

"I couldn't have done it without Guy. He gets most of the credit." Then a tear ran down Valerie's face. "I'm so glad she's okay. Can I see her? Can *we* see her?"

"Of course!" Both May and Chet spoke at once.

Chet reached for the door. "She's sleeping," he said. "Poor tot needs the rest."

"I'm not surprised," Valerie answered.

Stetson in hand, Guy followed the three of them into the room. Lizzie lay in a large raised crib with net topping over it. An IV ran into her arm.

"The IV will come out soon," May said. "Then we

can take her home. Plenty of food, the doctor said. That man didn't feed her enough."

Guy got his first good look at Lizzie. To think all this time he'd known her face only from photographs. She was even more adorable in life.

Adorable? That didn't sound like a word he'd usually use. Hah. This whole experience had changed him in unexpected ways.

He stood for a while, looking at the child whose plight had consumed him for so many days, and felt good about himself.

Then he moved quietly. "I need to get to the office. This case needs winding up."

Valerie hesitated. "I'd like to come along, Guy. I want to know everything."

He nodded. "Come on. And when we're done with this, I gotta find a way to help Etta."

Val followed him out the door. "You're right. It's wrong to leave her out there all by herself on the edge of poverty."

"It's wrong for a lot of people, but she did a great thing, didn't she?"

"It wasn't easy for her either." Val smiled. "Remarkable, when you think about all she's been through with that beast."

"She said it was the best thing she's done in her life." He didn't mention how glad Etta had been to see Phillip shot. No need to bring that up, not when it was probably raw for Val.

Phillip Margolis was still in the hospital, under

sedation, under guard. Not that the coward was likely to try anything, not when it might cost him his leg.

What they wanted were the rest of the details, details that might lock his prison cell even tighter.

And eventually they wanted to know why he'd chosen Lizzie Chamberlain to give to his wife, although they had a good idea about that. Still, they needed the creep to say it. To brag.

Guy suspected the man would brag quite a bit.

Valerie again looked out of place in the front squad room, as out of place as she had upon her arrival. But this time she was greeted with nods and smiles. Those who spoke called her *Detective*.

She had become a recognized part of the team. Guy wondered if she realized that.

After they'd wound up the paperwork with as much as they had learned, Guy suggested he drive Val home.

Once in the Suburban, she spoke wearily. "I want to hear that man tell it all. I want him to nail himself with his own mouth."

"Me, too," Guy agreed as he pulled up in front of the Chamberlain house. "A full confession."

"Yeah." Instead of climbing out of his vehicle, she leaned her head back and turned it to look at the house. "There's still one thing I want to know."

"What's that?"

"Why May never heard Lizzie cry."

The question slammed Guy. Val had mentioned it before, but he'd forgotten all about it during the hunt. Answers tended to come later when a case was solved.

"Yeah," he said reluctantly. "Yeah." But maybe neither of them truly wanted to know.

The question hung there like a huge loose end.

Then Val looked at him. "Can I come to your place, Guy?"

Chapter Twenty

"Sure," Guy answered, slipping his vehicle into gear. He tried to sound nonchalant but wasn't sure he succeeded. His heart began a slow, steady throbbing as he drove through town. It continued as they both exited the vehicle and headed for his apartment. The stairway had never seemed so long.

Inside, he asked her if she wanted coffee, or just to sleep.

She smiled faintly and gestured, the movement taking in the entire place. "You haven't committed, have you."

He stilled, surprised by the comment. "What do you mean?"

"Oh, you're committed to the job, all right. I've seen it. Total commitment."

"Then what?" He scanned his own apartment. Only partly furnished.

"I mean this place. You may be committed to your work, but you're not committed to staying here. Some part of you believes you'll be moving on. To what, Guy?"

He remained quiet as he looked around again. Maybe she was right. What did that mean about him?

"At home," she continued, "I have plenty of furniture. So I can entertain. So I can be comfortable all the time. I hung pictures on the wall. I have some appliances on my counter. It looks like a home, not a waystation." She studied him. "It's obvious you don't have friends come over. Do you feel you don't have any?"

He blew a long breath.

She looked into his eyes. "All you have on the walls is that beautiful blanket your mother made. Do you think about going home to your family all the time? Or something else? You don't feel permanent, do you?"

He felt stripped uncomfortably bare. He wanted to ignore her questions, dismiss them lightly. The problem was, there was truth in them. Maybe a truth he needed to face.

"I don't know," he said finally.

She shook her head and looked pained. "You've built walls around yourself. As clear as the boundaries of your reservation. You just don't believe you belong. You view everything through the lens of how you've been treated by Whites all your life."

He tried not to wince in response to words that struck him painfully. "Maybe so. With good reason."

She nodded, then sat on the edge of the recliner. "I'm sure you have reasons. You've shared some of them with me."

"So?"

"So maybe you need to commit yourself. To this county. To the place where you work and live your days. To the people around here. They can't *all* be jerks, can they?"

No, they weren't all jerks. Problem was that he was always steeling himself against meeting another one. They showed up. Boy, did they show up, and too many of them did it overtly.

But he was also trying to steel himself against Val, wasn't he? Wondering at some level what his family would think if he got more involved with her. Some of them already objected to him being a cop. How would they react to Valerie?

"Maybe," she said slowly, "you ought to wear the plainclothes you're entitled to wear now and stop worrying about the bigots. You know who *you* are. If they can't deal with it, tell them to shove it. You're a *detective* with the Conard County Sheriff's Department. Have more confidence in yourself. You deserve to."

He didn't know what to say. She didn't understand. Or maybe she understood more than he wanted to believe. He wanted to ask who she was to criticize him.

But deep inside he knew it was a critique he deserved. Maybe one he needed.

"Val..." But he didn't know what to say. Home truths. He needed to think about them. But Val didn't give him time, not then.

She smiled at him. "Take me to bed, Guy."

His head exploded as if light burst through him.

For a split second his world turned brilliant, so bright he couldn't see anything.

Then he took a long breath and reached for her hand. "Val, come with me."

"All the way, if you want." Her smile lingered as she took his hand and rose.

All the way? But he couldn't question her, not then. His pulse pounded through him, the desire for her that he couldn't ignore, that he no longer needed to ignore, rising in him as he led her to his bed.

"I hear the thunder," he said.

Her smile broadened. "Me, too."

SHE WAS EXQUISITE. Val didn't wait for him to undress her, but slowly shed her jacket, then reached for the buttons on her creamy blouse. Still smiling.

"You, too," she said huskily. "Or I'll do it myself."

He wouldn't have minded, but neither did he want wait.

All at once they sped up, clothes flying everywhere.

Falling together, they landed on the bed. Their hands began to move in a journey of discovery. Her skin was as smooth as silk and when she writhed against him, her hips rising, he felt the blaze rise in his own body along with zings of lightning.

Oh, he heard the thunder all right. It hammered in his ears, filling him with its power.

He caressed her breasts, their nipples pebbling beneath his fingers. He ran his hand down her side and finally reached her center. She arched against him, then closed her hand around his staff.

Her voice was breathless. "Now, Guy. Fill me now."

He couldn't have waited a second longer. Sliding into her hot wet depths felt as good as a homecoming. She moaned and tightened around him as her hips began the rhythm as old as time.

He rose and fell with her, riding the storm of desire. Higher and higher until at last thunder clapped a final time.

Together they found deep contentment. Deep satisfaction.

Together. As one.

THEY FELL ASLEEP, wrapped in his comforter, wrapped in each other's arms. Val had no idea how long she slept, but when she woke all she wanted to do was snuggle closer.

Guy. His warmth. His strength. His kindness. His determination. So much to admire.

Then there was his sexiness. She had to stifle a giggle for fear of waking him, of him pulling away. She squeezed her eyes closed, remembering their lovemaking. As far as she was concerned it had been perfect. She hoped he felt the same.

Desire had been running like a current all along, beneath her fear and anguish. Buried because it was out of place. The wrong time.

But the time was wrong no longer. She didn't want to think about what might come. About all the problems. Their jobs, so far apart. Their cultures creating a distance that wasn't measured in miles. Reasons for a new fear and she wasn't sure how she'd handle any of it.

But in these special moments, cradled against him, she pushed the worries aside. They'd arrive when they couldn't be ignored. Just accept the now. The gift.

GUY AWOKE TO the miracle of Val snuggled against him. He knew by her breathing that she no longer slept. He hugged her closer, aware that they'd opened a can of worms they wouldn't be able to ignore. He forced the thoughts away.

He shifted his head so that he looked into her face, seeing her drowsy smile. He wanted to keep that smile there forever.

Then his stomach growled loudly. She giggled.

"Embarrassing," he said, "but when was the last time we ate?"

She answered with certitude. "I had some dried cereal with Etta yesterday morning."

"For me it was during the night when I ate deer jerky."

"Too long," she agreed.

"I can run to the truck stop and get something. Or you can risk your life with whatever I might have lying around here. I don't cook for myself often."

"How about we both go to the truck stop? Sounds much safer to me. Easier, too." Then she laughed.

It was the most beautiful sound he'd ever heard, except maybe her moan of completion.

He jumped out of bed and grabbed for his clothes. "I'll beat you."

"Just you try."

Laughing like kids, they pulled on their clothes, more rumpled this time. He wore jeans and a sweatshirt. She pulled on her suit again.

The suit that announced another barrier.

Hell!

The drive to the truck stop diner didn't take long, and soon they were inside. Only then did Guy see the clock and realize it was 4:00 a.m. They'd gotten some real sleep.

Valerie ordered eggs, bacon, a side of home fries. Guy doubled the same order for himself.

They faced each other across a table in a booth. The dark night beyond the window was punctuated by rumbling trucks beneath vapor lamps. You couldn't see many stars from here.

All Guy wanted was to look at Valerie anyway. Beautiful had become gorgeous in his eyes. He wondered how she saw him, but from her smile decided her view of him couldn't be that bad.

The coffee was rich and dark, waking him up more. It appeared to have the same effect on Val as she held the mug in both hands.

After they were served and had eaten in silence for a few minutes, Val looked up from her plate.

"You know we're going to have things to talk about," she said with uncharacteristic uncertainty.

"Yes." Things he didn't want to talk about at all.

"That is," she continued, "if you don't want it to end here."

The words burst from him, barging past his usual restraint. "I *don't* want this to end here. Do you?"

She shook her head, looking down again. A sigh escaped her. "Maybe we can deal with one issue at a time."

"It's possible. Or we can deal with them all at once and let the straws fall where they may."

She looked up and her gaze locked on his face. "What do you mean?"

"I want to marry you." He spoke with conviction. "To hell with all the rest of it. We'll deal."

She stopped breathing. Her eyes widened. "Guy?"

"I mean it." He'd never meant anything more in his life. It had crashed in on him during the night just past. He wanted this woman forever under any terms. Now all he had to fear was her answer.

"Your family?" she asked quietly.

"They can live with it the same way they live with me being a cop. You were right. I need to stop erecting barriers. This one comes down *now*. I love you. Will you marry me?"

Her face suddenly glowed like a rising sun. "Yes, Guy. Oh, yes. Come what may." Then, "I love you, too."

He smiled the broadest smile he had in ages. He felt like he was walking on air.

Then, just to keep himself under control, he said, "Finish eating or I'm going to drag you out of here right now. The bed might still be warm."

She laughed, a pure, clear sound. "What a difficult choice. You're impossible."

He laughed, too. God, had he nearly forgotten how to laugh?

REALITY RETURNED AS it always did. Morning came too soon. Bright sunlight filled the world, for once not feeling like an affront.

Guy swung Val by the Chamberlain house to clean up and change. Again she emerged wearing one of her suits. Today it didn't feel like the barrier it had seemed just last night.

She'd agreed to marry him. It didn't get better than that.

When she slid into his Suburban, she said, "They aren't home from the hospital yet. I should check in on Lizzie."

"Absolutely."

She chewed her lip as they drove. "I think it's too soon to question May."

He thought about it, dreading the answer she might get. "Yeah, give her a day or two to get used to having Lizzie back. Maybe it's not really important." He ached for Val in expectation of the pain she might soon feel.

"It's important," she answered. "I *have* to know."

THE CHAMBERLAINS WERE still at the hospital, both of them in Lizzie's room. Nobody tried to halt Val or Guy, to limit the number of visitors.

May and Chet looked weary but happy. Lizzie still slept.

"How is she?" Valerie asked.

"She's fine," May answered with a smile.

The IV was gone, Valerie noted. A good sign. A good sign that Lizzie slept so peacefully.

"A few more hours," Chet said. "Then we'll take her home."

We. Valerie noticed that but didn't want to press. Were her sister and her husband patching it up? Coming together again? She hoped so. She'd always liked Chet, had always believed until two years ago that May had made the right decision in marrying him. She wanted to see that contentment in May again.

Chet rose and extended his hand to Guy. "I haven't thanked you yet."

Guy returned the handshake but shook his head the tiniest bit. "No thanks necessary. I wanted Lizzie safely home as much as you did."

Then Chet turned to Valerie and hugged her. "You came when May needed you. I'll always be grateful to you."

As if she could have done anything else, Val thought as she returned his hug. Was Chet beginning to realize that he hadn't been there enough when he was needed before?

May spoke. "Chet is going to let Lucy handle more of the workload."

Chet nodded as he stepped back. "Belatedly it occurred to me that Lucy isn't the only one with a family to care for."

So he *was* thinking about it. Reordering his priorities. "Good for you," was all Val answered. About time, too.

She let her question go for now. In a day or two, when the Chamberlains had settled back in together, she'd ask. She needed to know why May hadn't heard Lizzie cry. Maybe May had an answer. Or maybe the answer lay entirely with Margolis.

She summoned her patience, but it wasn't as hard as when Lizzie was missing.

SHE AND GUY went by the sheriff's office again and found a squad room looking weary but happy. They'd all exhausted themselves in the hunt for Lizzie and Valerie tried to thank them.

They were having none of it. "What?" asked Sarah Ironheart. "Like we'd have ignored it?"

Connie Parish laughed. "After we all catch up with some sleep we're going to throw a party. You gonna join us, Detective?"

"Call me Val. And yes, I'll be there."

Guy asked, "Where's Gage?"

"Emma made him come home," Mark Alton answered. "She worries about him."

"And Margolis?"

"Still knocked out. Doc says we might get some sense out of him tomorrow. Guess he lost a whole lot of blood."

Guy looked at Val. He saw her jaw tighten. No, she wasn't happy about shooting the man, much as he deserved it. He'd have wondered about her, though, if she didn't feel it. No one should ever be immune to that. To being responsible for pulling a trigger.

"I'm not even going to *try* to cook," Guy said as they emerged into the sunny day. "We've got better things to do. I'll ransack Maude's menu. How's that?"

That smile danced across Val's face again. "You make me happy, Guy."

As happy as she made him, he hoped.

LATER, THOUGH, WHEN they were sated with food, and temporarily with their hungry bodies, Val took the recliner and Guy pulled up one of his kitchen chairs, reaching for her hand.

"Well?" he asked reluctantly, unusual nerves filling him. "Changing your mind?"

"God no! But how are we going to do this? Who do we tell and when? What about your family? Our jobs?"

Guy looked down, facing the justice of her concerns. "I love you, Val. We've got to find a way."

"Yeah, we do." She leaned back and closed her eyes. "It's not enough to just let things fall where they may. I don't want you to be unhappy for any reason. But…"

"Yeah, but." He sighed. "Tell you what. We'll meet in the middle at some hotel or other when we can both get away."

She nodded slowly. "I want to get as much of you as I can. But there's no room for another detective here. And I don't think I can go back to patrol."

"No, of course not." He wouldn't ask that from her ever.

"And you can't move to Gunnison. Too far from your roots, your family, your people. I don't want that either." She needed her job and the sense of purpose he gave her. He'd even sacrifice himself to save her from losing that.

She opened her eyes. "We'll manage. I love you too much not to try."

"That's it then. Tomorrow you get May to answer your question. And I'll take a trip out to the rez. We'll go from there."

THE NEXT MORNING, Guy dropped Val off at the Chamberlain house, then headed out to the rez. A satellite phone call had prepared the way for him.

At the Chamberlain house, happiness filled the air. Lizzie was curled in her father's arms, viewing her world from her safe vantage point. Val managed to hold the little girl for a few minutes before her crying became too much.

She grinned. "That crying must have driven Margolis crazy."

May laughed. "I hope so."

But the moment had come. Every inch of Val's body tightened. God, she didn't want to do this. "May, can I have a few private words?"

May looked at her sister, her smile fading. "Sure, Val."

They went into the master bedroom and closed the door. May had grown stiff, her hands tightening, her gaze on her sister. "What's wrong, Val? What's wrong?"

Valerie drew a deep breath, hating the words she was about to speak. "May, why didn't you hear Lizzie cry the night she was taken?"

May dropped down onto the edge of the bed, her face paling. "Oh, God, Val." Then she started crying quietly.

Val promptly sat beside her and wrapped her arm around her sister's shoulders. "May, I'm sorry. I have to know, just for me. No one else needs to. No one else is wondering." Except she'd share whatever it was with Guy. She wasn't about to start anything by lying to him.

Tears dribbled down May's face. "I'm awful. Just awful."

"How so?"

"I had a few drinks. Some nights I'd have a few just so I could sleep. But Lizzie's cries always woke me up. *Always.* I swear."

"But that night was different. How?"

May put her hands over her face. "Oh, God!"

"May?"

May scrubbed her face with her sleeve. "Oh, all right! I didn't drink. I took sleeping pills. Prescription sleeping pills! I started doubling the dose."

Valerie felt shock all the way to her toes. "May…"

"I'm awful, just awful!"

Val hugged May even tighter. "You've got to stop that before you get addicted."

"I know. I know! I'll never touch them again, I swear."

But now Val had another question even as she ached for May. "Did anyone know that you did that regularly?"

May wiped her face. "A few. I was worried about it, so I told some of my friends."

And that explained a whole lot, Valerie thought. *The grapevine.* The one little piece of information that no one had shared out of loyalty to May. Because it seemed irrelevant to Lizzie's disappearance.

Only it hadn't been. Not that it would have helped much in finding Lizzie.

She held May, rocking her gently. "It's okay. It'll be okay now. If you need help, ask Chet. Please."

May nodded. "I will. I promise I will. Maybe I should have taken those antidepressants he wanted me to. God, this whole mess has been terrible. Postpartum depression then this. I can't blame anyone but me."

"I wouldn't say that at all. There's no one to blame but Phillip Margolis. No one."

With her eyes closed, Val wondered though. If May had awakened and found Margolis in her house, with her baby? Matters might have taken an even worse turn.

Gray Cloud waited for Guy in his small shed on the side of Thunder Mountain. A foothold he retreated to for peace, to keep an eye on the mountain. It was an infrequent break from tribal councils and other matters that needed the attention of an elder.

Gray Cloud sat cross-legged by a fire, a tin coffeepot resting on the rocks that made the fire ring. He smiled and waved Guy to sit with him. "It's a beautiful day. Coffee?"

Guy accepted. A strong, rich brew with a few stray coffee grounds in it. As near as he could tell, Gray Cloud had never abandoned all the old ways. A keeper of the tribe's history and wisdom.

"So," said Gray Cloud, his dark gaze kind. "What brings you?"

"You've been more of a father to me than my real one."

Gray Cloud nodded. "Sometimes that's the way of it. I gather you have a knotty problem you want to discuss?"

Guy chuckled. "I came knocking, didn't I?"

"It's usually why. I might not be able to help. I'm not the smartest man on the earth, you know."

"I wouldn't expect you to be." He remained silent and so did Gray Cloud. He let the heat and richness of the coffee pour through him as he enjoyed the peace of the woods around him. A squirrel hopped by, unafraid.

"Okay," Guy said presently. "I want to marry Valerie Brighton."

"Why would that be a problem?"

"My family. You must know they don't approve of me being a cop. They're going to disapprove even more about this."

Gray Cloud raised an eyebrow. "You played with my children when you were young."

Guy nodded. He vividly remembered those childhood days. Days of freedom and fun, the bunch of them running around, playing games.

"And you knew their mother," Gray Cloud said.

Guy remembered Gray Cloud's wife, too. A wildlife biologist who had come to Thunder Mountain to study wolves. She had died too young. "But you know my family, what they're like."

"You know that my wife was non-Native. The disapproval didn't stop me. Will that stop you?"

Guy waited, sensing there was more. Some reminder he wanted.

"I don't know everything, Guy, but I know one thing."

"What's that?"

"No man has the right to decide the course of another man's life. Follow your heart. But you didn't need me to tell you that."

Maybe he *hadn't* needed to hear it, Guy thought, but he still felt better when he went down the mountain to meet his parents. An elder hadn't disapproved. Now his parents could just deal with it.

They'd have to anyway.

VAL AND GUY met again late that afternoon at his apartment. She burst with curiosity. "How'd it go?"

Guy nodded. "It went. Gray Cloud gave his blessing."

"Would that have made a difference?"

He smiled. "Nope. But it was still good to hear from a man who's like a father to me."

"I'm sure it was. You're still very much a part of your people. Besides, it's always good to feel that people we care about aren't against us. And your parents?"

Now he laughed. "About what I expected. As if I'd taken a dump on the doorstep. They'll get used to it. Or they won't." He shrugged. "I knew what I was going to do and nothing would have stopped me. Bottom line."

"Like becoming a cop."

"Like becoming a cop," he agreed. "Now you. What did you learn?"

"Oh, it wasn't good." Her face saddened and she perched on the recliner. "Damn it, Guy, get another decent chair. This is ridiculous."

He grinned. "I hear you, Detective Thunder. What about May?"

Sorrow whispered over her face. "This is a secret, Guy. Totally."

"Lips sealed and all that. Tell me."

"May's been taking sleeping meds. Doubling the dose."

He dragged the kitchen chair over and sat as close as he could get, his concern for Val deepening until it nearly hurt. "Other people knew?"

"Evidently she got worried enough to tell some friends. After that, I suppose one of them mentioned it outside the small group and the grapevine did its work. Margolis must have heard."

"That would explain a lot. How's May doing?"

"Feeling ashamed. Blaming herself. I told her she needs to talk to Chet. I hope she does."

"Sounds like she's going to need some help."

"Yeah." She sighed. "Yeah."

Eventually she shook her head. "Let's get back to us, Guy. I want to feel the happiness and love you give me. I want to get rid of the rest of the whole damn world, at least for now."

In total agreement, he scooped her up and carried her toward the bed. She laughed at last.

"The grapevine's working again already," he murmured huskily. "Guaranteed."

"Then let them talk. They'll just be full of envy."

He laid her down, then sank beside her, hugging her close. "I love you, Detective Valerie Brighton."

"I love you, too, Detective Guy Redwing. Forever."

"Forever won't be long enough."

* * * * *

#2157 MAVERICK DETECTIVE DAD
Silver Creek Lawmen: Second Generation • by Delores Fossen

When Detective Noah Ryland and Everly Monroe's tragic pasts make them targets of a vigilante killer, they team up to protect her young daughter and stop the murders. But soon their investigation unleashes a series of vicious attacks...along with reigniting the old heat between them.

#2158 MURDER AT SUNSET ROCK
Lookout Mountain Mysteries • by Debra Webb

A ransacked house suggests that Olivia Ballard's grandfather's death was no mere accident. Deputy Detective Huck Monroe vows to help her uncover the truth. But as dark secrets surrounding Olivia's family are exposed, she'll have to trust the man who broke her heart to stay alive.

#2159 SHROUDED IN THE SMOKIES
A Tennessee Cold Case Story • by Lena Diaz

Former detective Adam Trent is stunned to learn his cold case victim is alive. But Skylar Montgomery is still very much in danger—and desperate for Adam's help. Their investigation leads them to one of Chattanooga's most powerful families...and a vicious web of mystery, intrigue and murder.

#2160 TEXAS BODYGUARD: WESTON
San Antonio Security • by Janie Crouch

Security Specialist Weston Patterson risks everything to keep his charges safe. But protecting wealthy Kayleigh Delacruz is his biggest challenge yet. She doesn't want a bodyguard. But as the kidnapping threat grows, she'll do anything—even trust Weston's expertise—to survive.

#2161 DIGGING DEEPER
by Amanda Stevens

When Thora Graham awakens inside a coffin-like box with no memory of how she got there, Deputy Police Chief Will Dresden, the man she left fifteen years ago, follows the clues to save her life. Their twisted reunion becomes a race against time to stop a serial killer's vengeful scheme.

#2162 K-9 HUNTER
by Cassie Miles

Piper Comstock and her dog, Izzy, live a solitary, peaceful life. Until her best friend is targeted by an assassin. US Marshal Gavin McQueen knows the truth— a witness in protection is compromised. It's dangerous to recruit a civilian to help with the investigation. But is the danger to Piper's life...or Gavin's heart?

HARLEQUIN
PLUS

Try the best multimedia subscription service for romance readers like you!

Read, Watch and Play.

Experience the easiest way to get the romance content you crave.

Start your **FREE TRIAL** at
<u>www.harlequinplus.com/freetrial</u>.